She stopped. By now tears had filled her eyes and her heart felt as if it might break. She truly believed that God had heard her prayer. What she did not know was whether or not he would grant her request. Against great odds, God had given her a new heart when she'd desperately needed one. And he had brought Josh into her life as well. She believed that with all her heart and soul. Now there was nothing more she could do except wait. And have faith.

Katie lifted her arms in the moonlight in supplication to the heavens.

REACH
for
TOMORROW

ONE LAST WISH

Lurlene McDaniel

REACH
for
TOMORROW

BANTAM BOOKS
NEW YORK • TORONTO • LONDON • SYDNEY • AUCKLAND

RL 5.7, ages 10 and up

REACH FOR TOMORROW

A Bantam Book/August 1999

ISBN 0-553-57109-5

Published simultaneously in the United States and Canada.

Bantam Books are published by Bantam Books, a division of Random
House, Inc. Its trademark, consisting of the words "Bantam Books" and
the portrayal of a rooster, is Registered in U.S. Patent and Trademark
Office and in other countries. Marca Registrada. Bantam Books, 1540
Broadway, New York, New York 10036.

PRINTED IN THE UNITED STATES OF AMERICA
OPM   10 9 8 7 6 5 4 3 2

Dear Reader,

Welcome to the world of One Last Wish. It is a world of many interconnected lives—people who are sick, as well as people who are healthy. All of them are full of dreams and hopes. One Last Wish is about reaching out and making a difference—even a small one that has lasting value for someone else.

In this book you'll meet characters who have appeared in some of my earlier works, but this story stands alone. The people you'll meet have been touched by the One Last Wish philosophy, which helps those who are facing life's difficulties to find meaning in acts of kindness and courage. Think of a pebble that is dropped into a calm lake. From the tiny pebble, concentric circles ripple outward, growing larger until they touch the shore.

As you join me in the world of One Last Wish, you'll meet not only teens who confront difficult problems, but also people who see beyond their own limitations and their own suffering. Share their pain as well as their hope and discover in yourself an appreciation of all that life offers. Just as the ripples spread out far around the pebble, the actions you choose to take have an impact, even if you do not see it. Once you show the world you care, you will find yourself looking into the heart of love.

Sincerely,

ONE

Dear Katie,

I'm writing to you, as well as to several others, with some exciting news. The JWC Foundation is rebuilding Jenny House. There was no way I could allow anything to do with Jenny Crawford, including her grandmother's dream to create a tribute to her granddaughter, to die, especially through something so horrific as a freak fire. So, with insurance funds, generous donations from "angels," and the help of the Foundation itself, we're rebuilding.

Which brings me to the purpose of this letter. While the actual facility won't be ready by this summer, I still want to sponsor the camp for the children who need it the most—those stricken with diseases and medical problems. The group will be smaller this year, but we've already built cabins and a log rec center in the woods, down near the stables. I have a small but brilliant medical staff hired, and now all I need are counselors for each cabin—four women, two men. I'd like you to be one of those women. . . .

Katie O'Roark stopped reading long enough to glance at the calendar pinned to her dorm room bulletin board.

"What's up?" asked her college roommate, Tara Greene. "You're smiling." Like Katie, Tara was on athletic scholarship, but Tara's was for swimming. They had arrived as freshmen in the fall and were now wrapping up their last few weeks before final exams. They'd already decided to be roomies when they returned as sophomores.

"A summer job in North Carolina," Katie answered.

"What!" Tara jumped down from the top bunk and snatched the letter from Katie's hands. "Not fair! I have to live at home and flip burgers all summer. How did you luck out?"

Katie grabbed the letter back. "It's that counselor job I told you about from last summer."

"You told me the place burned."

"They're rebuilding."

"Are you taking the job?"

"I'd like to. My folks won't be too thrilled. They wanted me home all summer, but how can I say no? I'll bet Mr. Holloway asks some of my friends to work there too. Maybe I can get you on staff."

"No way. I couldn't stand being around sick kids. It would break my heart."

"You're around me."

"A heart transplant doesn't count. And besides, look at all the track medals you won this season. How can you *ever* think of yourself as sick?"

A string of Katie's medals lined her bulletin board, and at the campus gym, the display case housed two trophies with her name engraved on them.

"How can you find out if he asked your friends?" Tara asked.

"I can e-mail Chelsea and Lacey and ask, of course." Katie read the rest of the letter. "Mr. Holloway says he's asking a few others who were helped by the JWC Foundation, but he doesn't say exactly who. It's helped plenty of people, so I wouldn't expect to know them anyway."

"Maybe your old boyfriend, Josh, will be asked."

Katie's heart skipped a beat. She hadn't thought of that. In truth, she hadn't been looking forward to going home to Ann Arbor because she knew she'd have to face Josh Martel. They'd broken up the summer before at Jenny House, and things hadn't gone well between them at Christmas break. Josh said he still loved her, but she didn't know how she felt about him anymore. She was grateful for all he'd been in her life. He had nothing to do with his parents, both alcoholics, and had pretty much been on his own since his brother's death. In fact, when Katie had gotten her transplant, it had been Josh's brother's heart that had replaced her own. Knowing that she had contributed to Josh's unhappiness, but still had his brother's heart beating inside her, only made Katie feel guilty. Katie wanted a fresh start in college. Except that college had been a lot of studying and hard work, and no guy had come along to take Josh's place.

"If Josh gets asked, I guess I'll deal with it," Katie said. "But I know that ever since his grandfather died and left him the house, Josh has had to stick close to home. So he probably won't have time to work at camp all summer." She didn't add that he was also a student at the University of Michigan and working to pay the bills.

"Well, even if he doesn't go, maybe there'll be a guy who'll appeal to you. You're awfully picky, you know."

"I'm not either." Katie sniffed. "I just have high standards."

"If you want my opinion, I think you still have feelings for Josh."

Katie felt her Irish temper flare. "Well, I don't want your opinion, thank you very much."

Tara feigned innocence. "You protest too much."

Katie flung a paper clip at her. "Go study for your Shakespeare test and forget about my love life, all right?"

Tara caught the clip in midair. "If you don't want him, girl, show my picture to him, will you? Good guys are hard to find, and from all you've told me about Josh, he sounds like a dream."

Katie buried her nose in the letter from Mr. Holloway. *Summer camp!* She could hardly wait. And if Josh was there, she'd manage. They could just be friends. That would be simple enough. Wouldn't it?

"Actually, Megan, I think taking this camp job would be a good idea . . . especially since you want to go on to medical school. It's only eight weeks out of the summer. It'll be a good experience."

Meg Charnell listened to her father's advice without enthusiasm. Her first year of college had been hard work, and she'd been looking forward to a summer of doing nothing. But then the letter had arrived with the offer to work at a camp for sick children. "How did this Mr. Holloway get my name, anyway?"

"I suspect that your days of being a candy striper and volunteer helper have been noticed. His foundation networks with all the big hospitals. It's a very philanthropic organization. That was the organization that helped the Jacoby boy, you know."

Donovan Jacoby. How could she ever forget? Megan had met him the first summer she had been a candy striper. He had been a patient at the hospital, waiting for a liver transplant. A new liver had not arrived in time to save his life.

The anonymous donor, JWC, had given Donovan $100,000, and he had passed it along to his divorced mother. She still lived in and managed the house that the money had gone to remodel. Families stayed there while their sick children were undergoing prolonged treatments at the giant hospital where Meg's father practiced surgery. Except that even Dr. Charnell's considerable skill hadn't been able to save Donovan Jacoby. But, she reminded herself, knowing Donovan had kindled her own dream to become a pediatrician.

"Maybe you're right," she said, taking back the letter. "Maybe I should go. I'm just not crazy about going someplace where I don't know a soul."

"You'll make friends," her father said. "And as a

counselor, you'll meet others your age. I'm sure they're only asking the brightest and best to act as counselors. And that's my girl: the brightest and the best."

"Oh, Dad. You're saying that because you're my father."

"Not true. How many college freshmen can say they aced all their courses in their first year at Columbia? Not many!" he answered his own question. "You'll be a terrific doctor one day."

Never in a million years would Meg have thought she'd be interested in medicine after growing up with a father who was always on call, busier with his patients and their concerns than those of his own family. But her feelings had changed once she'd met Donovan. "I'll think about camp." She leaned down and kissed her father's cheek. "Now, how about taking me to dinner? Mom's got one of her committee meetings, so we're on our own tonight."

Later Meg called her friend Alana and told her about the job offer. "I don't suppose you got a letter too," she said hopefully.

"I couldn't have gone even if I'd wanted to," Alana told her. "Remember? I'm headed to Europe with my church choir at the end of June."

"Oh, yeah, that's right." Meg felt disappointed. Ever since they'd been candy stripers together, she and Alana had been friends, and even though she'd been away at Columbia and Alana was attending a two-year college near Washington, D.C., they both had the same dreams—to practice medicine one day.

"But I still think you should go," Alana said. "It sounds like a great opportunity to be around sick kids. And isn't that always the best way to find out if you're serious about pediatrics as a specialty?"

"Of course." Meg let out a sigh. "I know you're right. But so long, summer by the pool with a stack of brain-candy books for entertainment."

"You can read in your spare time, and most of these camps have lakes and water sports."

"And let the world see me in a bathing suit? Are you crazy?"

"You're too hard on yourself."

"You've heard of the freshman fifteen, haven't you? Well, I got my fifteen extra pounds and somebody else's too."

"You look fine."

"I know the truth, Alana." Meg's friend was tall and slim. How could she know what it was like to always feel overweight? "One good thing," Meg added. "There will be nobody at camp but kids, so they won't care if I'm fat."

"Male counselors," Alana said with authority. "Don't forget about them."

Meg sighed. She hadn't had a real date the entire school year, and most guys wanted to be her "friend" anyway. "Maybe they'll all be ugly."

"And maybe, just maybe, there will be a prince among the frogs."

"He won't notice me," Meg said quietly. She knew she wasn't beautiful. And she was too smart and too heavy for guys to notice. No guy except Donovan had ever shown any interest in her. And he was gone forever.

She hung up, knowing she would take the job. It would beat sitting around feeling sorry for herself all summer. And if there were cute guys at the camp she'd simply ignore them. No use wishing for something she couldn't have.

TWO

This is one dumb idea! Morgan Lancaster told himself as he surveyed the stable in the North Carolina woods. Why had he ever agreed to take this summer job at a camp full of sick kids in the first place?

Because of Anne Wingate, his inner voice answered before he even had time to get to the first stall. When the letter had arrived offering him the job as riding instructor and stable hand for the summer, he'd thought it seemed like a good idea. Normally he spent summers on the rodeo circuit or working on his aunt's ranch taking in tourists, although he hadn't done that since the summer he'd met Anne there. When Anne had arrived at the ranch she'd seemed like all the other wealthy tourists. But he'd soon realized that she was not like anyone else he had ever known. Anne was HIV-positive. After she'd left the ranch, Morgan had followed her back to her home in New York and stayed with her until she died. They were the most special and memorable days of his life, and they had changed him forever. Now here he was, twenty years old, volunteering for the summer, and feeling directionless.

A roan mare stuck her head out of the upper half of the stall door, and Morgan rubbed her muzzle. "How you doing, girl? Ready for a summer full of twelve-year-olds?"

The mare snorted and nuzzled his hand. Morgan could tell by the white hair around her nose and mouth that she was old. But she was also calm and seemed to have a sweet disposition. Perfect for kids and a far cry from the wild broncos he was used to working with.

In all, there were seven horses in the stable, each of them docile and good-natured. Taking care of them would be a piece of cake—if he didn't die of boredom. The first staff meeting was the following night. All day, counselors, nurses, physical therapists, and workers had been arriving. He'd seen some cute girls, but only from a distance. He wasn't interested in anyone. Nor had he been, ever since he'd lost Anne. Smart, pretty Anne. She'd been one in a million.

And she'd left him the money for the medical test. The test he still hadn't taken three years later. The test that would tell him once and for all whether he would get the debilitating disease Huntington's chorea. "Anne would kill me," he told the horse ruefully. "She'd say, 'Honestly, Morgan, how can a guy like you ride wild horses, almost getting his brains knocked out, and be afraid of a little test?'"

He *was* afraid. As long as he didn't know the truth, he didn't have to spend his life waiting for his genetic fate to take over his body . . . as it had his father's.

"You always talk to horses?"

Morgan spun to see another guy staring at him. The kid was taller than Morgan. "Easier than talking to people," Morgan admitted.

The other boy laughed. "I'm Eric Lawrence. Cook, groundskeeper, any old thing they need me to be."

"You get a letter too?"

"No. My sister, Christy, is a respiratory therapist. She's working here for the summer and dragged me along so I'd stay out of trouble." He grinned. "How about you?"

Morgan explained his job briefly, then asked,

"You okay about being around a bunch of sick kids?"

"It turns me off, but I had a couple of friends once—they had cystic fibrosis."

"Had?"

"Yeah. Kara died about three years ago. My buddy Vince died last winter. CF is a lung disease, you know. He died from pneumonia."

"My friend died from pneumonia too," Morgan said. He didn't add that Anne had also been a victim of AIDS.

"Tough way to go," Eric said. "Not being able to breathe and all. Anyway, because of the two of them, I said I'd come and help out. Do whatever needs doing . . . keep the kids away from the construction site. You been down there yet? It's going to be some place once they finish it."

They were to walk down to the site the next night after the get-acquainted meeting. The kids weren't arriving for two more days, but there was plenty to do before they got there. "Are you a good cook?" Morgan asked.

"Will it make a difference?"

Morgan laughed. "I've eaten some pretty bad camp grub, so I reckon not."

"Well, don't worry. There's a full-time dietician

on staff. I'm just a helper." Then Eric changed the subject. "Seen any of the girls yet? A few of them are babes."

"Haven't had time." Morgan hedged his reply.

"Make time. Then maybe we can really make this summer count."

Morgan wasn't quite sure just how to take Eric. *Young and cocky,* he thought. From down the line, a horse whinnied. "I'd better pitch out the stalls," Morgan said, remembering that he had work to do.

"I got stuff to do too. Catch you later."

Morgan watched Eric walk away. For the hundredth time in the past two years, he wished he could talk to Anne. She understood people. Morgan never had much patience with them. He preferred horses. But Anne was gone, and a dark cloud hung over his life. *No time for girls,* he told himself. And besides, caring for someone again before he had the test performed wasn't really very fair, now, was it?

"Where is everybody, and where's the marching band to greet me?"

"Lacey!" Katie jumped up from where she'd been sitting on the cabin floor, cutting out name tags, and ran to the screen door.

Chelsea James followed on her heels. The three girls hugged and squealed, all talking at once.

"Come in and meet Megan—Meg—she's a counselor too. This is the infamous Lacey Duval," Katie said, "the one we've been telling you about."

Lacey sized up the girl in front of her. "Not another blonde," she cried. "And a pretty one too. Didn't anybody tell her the rules? No blondes but me!"

Taken aback, Meg smiled. Could the tall, cool, beautiful Lacey she'd heard so much about all afternoon possibly think she, Meg, was pretty? Or was Lacey being nice?

"Lacey means what she says," Katie told Meg. "And she says *exactly* what she means."

Lacey sniffed haughtily and threw her suitcase to one side. "Are we all here?"

"Even Dullas," Chelsea said. "Kimbra brought her. We sent her off to pester somebody else."

"Who are Kimbra and Dullas?" Meg asked.

"Kimbra is one of the administrators on staff here. She was actually a friend of Jenny Crawford's. As for Dullas, well, you'll meet her later."

Katie peered through the screen door. "Did Jeff bring you?" she asked Lacey.

"Jeff is Lacey's boyfriend," Chelsea informed Meg. "They were both counselors at Jenny House last year."

"He couldn't bring me," Lacey said. "He got a

job working at an architectural firm. And since that's his major, he thought it was a good place to spend the summer. I drove myself."

"You drove all the way from Miami by yourself?" Chelsea asked.

Katie knew Chelsea was notorious for being fearful, but when you had been sick and in need of a heart transplant for as long as Chelsea had before getting one, it was easy to forgive her anxiety.

"It's only a two-day drive. I spent the night with my aunt in Jacksonville."

The group flopped onto the floor and Lacey asked, "So, Chelsea, what do you hear from DJ?"

Chelsea's face went sad. "He'll never care about me. He can't get over what happened to his sister."

Katie explained briefly to Meg how Chelsea and Jillian had both needed the same organ transplant, and that Chelsea had gotten it, while Jillian had died waiting for it.

Instantly Meg felt sorry for Chelsea. "The same thing happened to a friend of mine," she said. "He died waiting for a liver transplant."

There was a moment of heavy silence. "This conversation has gotten far too serious," Lacey said briskly. "Well, I'm sure there'll be other guys, Chelsea. It's DJ's loss." She turned to Katie. "I saw Josh when I pulled in. Did you know he was here, Katie?"

Katie's stomach did a flip-flop. "No."

"You mean you didn't see him while you were at home? You haven't talked to him since you got back from college?"

"I—uh—I've been busy."

"Too busy to see Josh?" Lacey looked incredulous.

"No way," Chelsea added.

"I'm not his keeper, you know," Katie said.

Lacey turned to Meg. "He's the nicest guy in the whole world. And they're perfect for each other. And someday our little Katie is going to wake up and realize it. We all just hope it won't be too late."

Katie jumped up. "Give it a rest." She went for the door. "See you all later. I'm going for a run."

"You can run, but you can't hide," Lacey called after her as she bolted through the doorway.

Furious at her friends' meddling, Katie jogged down one of the trails. Why couldn't they understand how mixed up she was inside about Josh? They were right, however. She hadn't called him while she'd been at home. And she'd left without ever letting him know she'd been there.

She picked up speed, realizing how much better

she always felt when she ran. For a while after she
had learned about the virus in her heart, she had
thought she might not survive, let alone run again.
But the heart transplant had given her back the
world she had been in danger of losing. She was
grateful every day to the One Last Wish Foundation, which had made it all possible.

She rounded a bend at full speed and ran smack
into a male chest.

"Whoa!" she heard the owner of the chest say. He
caught her arms to keep her from falling.

Katie looked up to see Josh's beautiful blue eyes
looking straight into hers.

THREE

"You're still as fast as the wind, aren't you, Katie?"

A lump in her throat almost prevented her from speaking. "I'm sorry," she said.

"Sorry for what?"

"Sorry for almost knocking you down," she said, but she meant it in many other ways.

He smiled. "Hey, I'm tough. I can take it."

"And I'm sorry because I didn't call you while I was home last week."

He studied her face, released her arms. "The phone works both ways, Katie. I could have called you too, but I didn't."

She didn't know why he would have wanted to; she hadn't been very pleasant to him. "I guess that's true."

He offered his lopsided smile. "Don't think I've

been sitting around pining away. I got your message last summer and at Christmas that you wanted to move on with your life and that the advancement didn't include me."

She started to protest, but he held up his hand. "It's all right; no hard feelings. We had a wonderful time together while it lasted. Maybe it's time both of us moved on."

"Are you seeing somebody else?" The question was out before she could stop herself.

"I'm dating someone, yes."

The news startled her and gave her a sick sensation in the pit of her stomach. She should feel glad for him. Wasn't this what she'd wanted? For them both to go their separate ways? "That's good," she said with a smile she didn't mean. This wasn't the time to remind him that only at Christmas he'd told her he still loved her.

"How about you? Anyone special out there in Arizona?"

"Um—not really. College was harder than I expected, and then with track and all . . ." She let the sentence trail off, remembering all the mornings he'd met with her after her transplant, encouraging her to run again. He'd hold the stopwatch, time her, cheer for her—

"I know what you mean." He interrupted her

thoughts. "But at least I'm going to college. Gramps left me enough for my first two years, if I'm careful. Maybe by the time I'm an upperclassman, I can get some scholarship money."

"Well, if hard work is a determinant, then I'm sure you'll get it. I know how hard you work, Josh."

He smiled again. "I'm glad we ran into each other. I wasn't sure you'd appreciate me working here this summer, what with you not wanting to be around me and all, but the truth is, I can make more money doing this camp than I ever could working back home. Besides, it's more fun here too."

"She'll miss you, I'll bet."

"Who?"

"Your girlfriend."

His face reddened. "We'll write. We'll keep in touch."

Curiosity about Josh's new girl was eating at her, but Katie knew she couldn't start pumping him for information right here in the middle of the hiking trail. He might start thinking she cared more than she did. She and Josh were broken up. They were friends, not boyfriend and girlfriend anymore. "I—um—should get back, I guess."

"Me too," he said. "It's going to be a good summer, Katie."

"Yes, it will be."

"See you, then."

"Yeah, see you." She started jogging away from him. It was definitely over between them. Katie sighed. If that was true, why did she feel so empty inside?

"I can't tell you how glad I am to see all of you." Richard Holloway was talking.

Meg looked around the rec center, fascinated by the group that had gathered. She knew that many of them had been there before, but even she, a Jenny House first-timer, was caught up in the importance of the summer ahead, and in the camaraderie she'd already experienced. Katie, Chelsea, and Lacey had made her feel like a welcome addition to their team, and Meg wanted to be part of the team in every way.

Mr. Holloway's talk was preparing her for the days ahead. These weren't ordinary campers coming in, but special kids fighting diseases, sometimes fighting for their very lives. She recalled her days as a candy striper and realized these kids wanted the same things all of them did—to be accepted and liked for who they were. They already had strikes against them: They were different, set apart by illness. This camp was going to try to make them feel normal while never losing sight of the truth.

"If you have *any* question about a kid in your cabin, you come and tell one of the medical staff," Richard Holloway was saying. "We can't take chances. And we're only minutes from a first-class hospital. We're a lot smaller this year, but full, so you'll have plenty to do."

He went on to tell them the camp rules, then opened the floor to questions. He assigned campers to cabins, which were all named after birds. Meg would have six charges in her Sparrow Cabin. Katie was in charge of Bluejay Cabin, Chelsea of Lark Cabin, Lacey of Redbird Cabin; Katie's former boyfriend, Josh, who Meg thought was handsome, was in charge of Eagle Cabin. Another boy, Kevin, would watch over Hawk Cabin. Once all the information had been given out, Mr. Holloway announced, "Now we're going to take a little trek over to the construction site. The crew's knocked off for the day, but I do want you to see what we're doing over there. Then it's back here for a cookout, and to bed. Tomorrow the campers arrive, and it's going to be chaos."

Meg shuffled out with the other girls and fell into step for the walk to the site. Cool mountain air rustled the trees along the trail.

"You're new here, huh?"

Meg turned her head and saw the girl the others called Dullas. She was a small girl and wore a nose ring. "Yep. But I've worked in my hospital back home with sick kids for a few years."

"I hated it the first time I came, but I like it now. I got adopted in April. Kimbra's my new mom. Now I've got brothers and a sister down in Tampa."

"Lucky you. To get an instant family, I mean."

"My old man's in jail, and my mother split when I was just a kid. Kimbra took me home after camp last summer, and now I live with her. My last name's changed to Patterson too, so now I belong to them."

Meg was amazed that the girl felt no shyness about the most personal details of her life. "Lacey told me you have leukemia."

"Had," Dullas corrected. "I'm in remission, and I don't plan to ever let that disease get out to torment me again."

"You can do that? Just wish it away?"

"I can, and I have. For the first time in forever things are going good for me, and I ain't going to let stupid old cancer mess them up."

Meg laughed. "Good luck."

Dullas crossed her arms and bobbed her head. "It's called a positive attitude. And I got it."

Light glinted off a necklace around Dullas's neck,

and Meg commented on its beauty. Dullas's hand flew protectively to her throat. "It's a real diamond. It's an earring, but Kimbra had it put into a necklace for me so I could wear it always. I'm sort of in charge of taking care of it for a girl who died. I didn't know her, but Katie, Chelsea, and Lacey did. They told me to take care of it for her. I'm like, you know, its guardian."

Meg figured she'd ask the others about it later. And it hit her hard that this indeed was no ordinary camp—here campers could die. She said, "Well, I think it's beautiful, and it looks as if you've taken good care of it."

"It's my treasure," Dullas said proudly. "I'm going to wear it forever."

By now they were rounding a bend, and the construction site came into view. The building loomed out of the woods, its steel girders catching in the late-afternoon sun. The group stood in a hushed semicircle, looking at it. "It's like the phoenix," Meg said half to herself.

"The what?" a boy near her asked. His name tag read MORGAN. She knew he was in charge of the stables.

"An Egyptian bird from mythology," Meg explained. "It rose again from its own ashes after being burned up."

He looked at her so long that she began to feel self-conscious.

Good move, she told herself. *A guy notices you because you said something dumb.* Why couldn't she be cute like Lacey, who was wisecracking and making others laugh?

"You must read a lot," Morgan said.

"I love to read. Books have always been my friends." She could have bitten her tongue. Why was she saying such stupid things?

Mercifully Richard Holloway said, "Look at the structure to the right. It's brand new."

Meg looked and saw another building rising out of the woods. Already she could tell it would be different from the institutional-looking first structure.

"What's it going to be?" Katie asked.

"A chapel," Mr. Holloway said. "The Jenny Chapel."

FOUR

For a hushed moment, no one spoke. Mr. Holloway broke the silence by saying, "Come on, let's get a little closer."

The group walked to what would be the entrance of the building, where the smell of freshly cut wood permeated the air. Katie could see that the building was bow shaped, with an angled front that soared several stories into the North Carolina air.

"The front there, facing west"—Mr. Holloway pointed to the soaring beams—"will be a solid stained-glass window. Local artisans are creating it as we speak."

Katie felt chills go up her spine as she imagined it.

"There will be a freestanding stone altar made from Carolina granite and walls of pine fitted together like the bow of a ship. There will be pews on either side in wedge-shaped sections with an aisle down the center. All of the interior will emphasize the altar and window.

"In the back will be a spacious vestibule, and on the basement level, rooms for music playing, choir rehearsal, a library, and so on. I want this to be a chapel that's used year-round."

Katie was moved. The chapel would be yet another monument to Jenny Crawford, and to Richard Holloway's love for her. Jenny and Richard had fallen in love years before, but Jenny had been diagnosed with leukemia and had died when she was only a teenager. Since then Richard had devoted his life to keeping her memory alive and helping young adults like her, through Jenny House and the One Last Wish Foundation.

"I think it's fabulous," Lacey said.

"There will be memorial plaques on the walls of the vestibule for every kid coming through Jenny House who doesn't make it. I want these kids remembered. For all time."

Katie remembered the makeshift memorial she and her friends had created for Amanda, and the sense of closure and peace it had brought them. Mr. Holloway was right—no one should ever be forgotten.

"When will it be finished?" Josh asked.

"Not until late fall or early next spring, depending on the weather. It will be the jewel in the crown of this complex." Mr. Holloway's voice rose with pride. "But here's a warning. This site is off limits to the campers. Actually, they have no reason to even want to come over this way, since all the activity is planned on the far side of the property. Just make sure you do regular head counts, all right?"

They all agreed. Finally the group headed back to the rec center, where the aromas of grilling burgers and hot dogs made Katie's mouth water.

"Last one there is ugly," Dullas called, and started off at a dead run.

Others broke into a trot, except for Meg.

"You're just poking along," Morgan said, coming up beside her. "Aren't you hungry?"

"Do I look as if I've missed many meals?" Meg asked, then wondered why she had said it. Why emphasize the obvious?

"You look fine to me."

"You're kind."

"No, I'm not. I'm honest."

She blushed because she hadn't had a guy flirt with her for a year and didn't know how to act. "Well, Mr. Honest, you're going to miss your supper if you drag along with me."

"There'll be plenty. I met one of the cooks." He

told her he was from Colorado, and she told him where she was from. He remarked, "I liked what you said about the phoenix. I could see that, you know . . . this giant bird rising right up to the sky. I'll bet you're really smart."

"I get by," she said.

"You remind me of someone. She was real smart too."

"A librarian?"

He smiled. "A girl I once knew."

Meg hoped he wasn't going to start crying on her shoulder about some girl who'd dumped him. She wasn't in the mood to be his buddy. "Sounds serious," she said without much enthusiasm.

"It might have been."

"A poet said that once. Actually, the exact words are, 'for of all sad words of tongue or pen,/The saddest are these: "It might have been!" ' "

"She used to do that too—say poetry to me. I liked it."

This surprised Meg. He looked rugged and outdoorsy, not the poetry-loving type. "Poetry's pretty. I've always loved it."

"Emily Dickinson was her favorite."

"But I *love* her!" Meg cried. "And Edna St. Vincent Millay too. Do you know her work?" She didn't wait for his answer. "And how about the

Brownings? And Maya Angelou?" She stopped abruptly, realizing that he was looking at her with an amused expression. She felt her cheeks flame. "Uh—look, I've got to go." She started jogging away.

"Wait," he called. "I want to talk to you."

"Maybe later." Meg put her head down and dashed off as fast as her legs would carry her, feeling like a fool.

Minutes later she arrived at the rec room, where a CD player was blaring and everybody was already sitting down with plates in front of them. Why had she ever agreed to come? She didn't belong here. The other girls were friends, and they had an unshakable bond. Meg would always be the outsider.

"Burger or hot dog?"

She looked up into Eric's smiling face. "What?"

"I'm the cook," he said. "Can I fix you a burger or a hot dog?"

"A burger's fine."

"You look like you've lost your best friend."

She forced a smile. "Just a little overwhelmed."

"Hey, me too." At the sizzling grill, he flipped her a burger. "You're Megan, aren't you?"

"How do you know my name?"

"Your name tag." He pointed. She blushed. He said, "Actually, I've been wanting to meet you."

"Why?"

"Because it looks like me and you are the only normal people here."

"What does that mean?"

"Everybody's either been sick at some point, or had a transplant. . . . Geez, I feel out of place, you know? I'm *healthy*."

His expression made her laugh. "You have a point. I'm healthy too. And glad of it. Are you sure we're the only ones?"

He grinned disarmingly. "Well, maybe I exaggerated a little. I think that Josh guy has never been sick either."

"Um—how about Morgan, the stable keeper?"

Eric set Meg's burger on a bun and handed it to her. "I'm not sure. He keeps to himself. I've tried to talk to him some, but he's not real sociable."

"I hope he isn't sick," she said.

Meg glanced over her shoulder and saw Morgan standing against a wall, staring at her and Eric. She turned quickly.

Eric leaned down. "Why don't we go sit down and talk? I'd like to get to know you better."

For the second time in an hour, Meg felt surprised that a guy wanted to be with her. *Must be something in the air,* she told herself. "All right," she said to Eric.

They sat, ate, and talked, and she figured out quickly that Eric liked to laugh and to party. He had a serious side too, however, and got very quiet when he told her about the deaths of his two friends. It didn't take much for her to surmise that Kara had liked him, or that he had been turned off by the mere idea of her illness. "So, here I am," he finally said. "Working at a camp full of sick kids. I'm only doing it for Kara and Vince. Because they didn't deserve to die and because I should have tried harder with them while they were alive."

"It makes no difference how hard you try," Meg said. "I did all I could for Donovan, but in the end I couldn't save him. If it had been a kidney he needed, I could have donated one of mine to him. But it was a liver."

"You would have done that? Given away a kidney to save somebody?"

She nodded. "I would have."

Eric's grin split his face. "I'm sticking close to you all summer. Just in case."

She laughed. He was very easy to be with, not at all like Morgan of the brooding eyes. Yes, having fun with Eric would be a perfect way to balance the job she had ahead of her caring for sick children.

Minutes later Mr. Holloway stood and led them in singing rounds of "Oh, How Lovely Is the Eve-

ning." The male voices, deep and resonant, under-
scored the girls' sweet, lilting echoes. They sang the
song three times, then stood in reverent silence as
the notes floated off on the summer breeze. Tears
formed in Meg's eyes at the tender beauty of the
song as she thought about all the kids who'd never
see a lovely evening here on earth again.

FIVE

"Bluejays! Over here!" Katie stood in the rec
center holding a sign that announced the
name of her cabin in large, colorful letters. The center was complete bedlam as campers and their families milled around the check-in tables, sorted
through papers with the medical staff, ran to meet
returning friends, and searched for their counselors.
Piles of luggage, duffel bags, pillows, and keepsakes
grew on the floor around Katie's feet as one by one
the campers found her.

So far, so good, she thought. She was lucky. Her
six bunkmates were mostly older girls, twelve or
thirteen. The oldest was sixteen, a girl named Sarah
McGreggor who hadn't turned up yet. But Katie
had also inherited Dullas, who might make up for
five flawlessly nice girls. Although Katie had to admit, adoption and belonging to Kimbra's family had

calmed Dullas considerably. Dullas could actually be friendly, and her language had certainly cleaned up. Last summer, she would burst into a stream of cursing at the least provocation.

"Are you Katie?"

Katie looked down into the sweet face of a young girl. Her hair was the color of pale honey and fell straight to just below her ears. "Yes, I'm Katie. And you?"

"Sarah McGreggor."

Katie was shocked. This girl looked too young to be sixteen. Then she remembered being told that sometimes chemo treatments stunted a person's growth. "Welcome to Jenny House," Katie said.

"I'm not sure I even wanted to come," Sarah said. "Hope you don't mind hearing that."

"Not at all. I felt the same way the first year I came. And my friend Lacey . . . well, her folks dragged her. But we're all back, and this time we're counselors. I say that so you'll know what a special place we think it is."

Sarah glanced around the room. "But it looks like I'm the oldest one here besides you counselors. I know I don't look sixteen, but I am."

"You'll have a good time," Katie assured her.

Just then a little boy skidded to a halt beside

them. He looked as if he must be five or six. "Sarah, guess what? You get to ride horses! Dad took me down to the stables and there's these many horses!" He held up all his fingers.

"My brother, Richie," Sarah explained, a soft smile lighting her face.

"Actually there are only seven horses, but we do get to ride them," Katie said with a laugh. "We'll rotate cabins, so you'll ride every other day."

A girl strolled up. She was a head taller than Sarah. "My sister, Tina," Sarah said. "She's four-teen."

Katie thought she looked more mature than Sarah, and felt sorry for the older girl. Cancer had robbed Sarah of much already. "Hey," Katie said to Tina.

"I wish I was staying," Tina grumbled.

"It's not a vacation for me, Tina," Sarah said. "I'd much rather be at home, you know."

Tina looked pouty, but she didn't argue.

When it came time for the families to leave, Katie watched each of the Bluejay Cabin girls hug her parents goodbye. Richie looked as if he might cry, and Sarah bent to give him a hug. "It's just for a few weeks," she told him.

"Like when you go to the hospital?" he asked her.

"Same amount of time, different reason," Sarah told him.

Mrs. McGreggor took the little boy's hand. "Sarah's not going back to the hospital, remember, Richie? She's had her transplant, and she's better now."

Katie didn't like eavesdropping, but she couldn't help thinking that Sarah didn't look better. Katie was automatically reminded of her own appearance after her heart transplant surgery: gaunt and colorless. She had also experienced a period of rejection, followed by a long recuperation process. But as her body had accepted the transplant, she had begun to gain weight back and had felt more energetic. Perhaps the weeks at camp would work the same wonders for Sarah, filling out her thin frame and brightening her dull complexion. Katie hoped so.

The Bluejays marched in a line to the cabin, where their stuff had already been delivered by workers. Inside, the group scattered like ants, scrambling for bunks. "Why don't you bunk near me?" Katie said to Sarah, and pointed to the far end of the room.

"But that's the bunk I want," Dullas announced.

"I want Sarah to have it," Katie said politely but firmly.

"That's all right," Sarah said. "She can have it."

"No. I'm the counselor. I get to choose. Sarah gets that bunk."

Dullas shot Sarah a murderous look but didn't argue. *A miracle,* Katie thought.

But when Katie pulled everybody into a get-acquainted game, Sarah begged off. "I'd just like to rest," she said.

Katie didn't try to persuade her. She understood Sarah's reluctance. After all, Sarah was sixteen; the others were just kids to her. She was in a child's world when she didn't want to be. Katie vowed to make Sarah's time at the camp the best she could possibly give her. Whatever the petite teen had been through, it had changed her. Of that Katie was certain.

"Everybody ready?"

Morgan's deep voice was answered by squeals and choruses of "Yes, yes!"

Meg appreciated her girls' enthusiasm; it was her cabin's turn to go horseback riding. She hadn't seen Morgan since camp started three days before, but just a look from him could turn her insides to jelly.

"Are they safe?" Meg asked, giving the saddled and waiting horses a skeptical eye.

"Perfectly tame and safe," Morgan assured her. "They know the trail by heart. Even if you drop the reins, each horse will tag along after the other, go so far, then turn around and come back. You couldn't get lost if you tried."

"You won't be coming along?"

"You're their fearless leader," he said.

She looked up and saw a hint of teasing in his expression. She colored. "Then I'll try not to embarrass myself."

"Ms. Meg." Nine-year-old Cammie tugged on her arm. "I have to go to the bathroom."

Meg rolled her eyes.

"Use the one in the tack room," Morgan said. "I'll get the others up on their mounts."

Meg ushered Cammie down the line of stalls and into the small room where saddles were kept. While the girl went to the rest room, Meg took a leisurely look around. The room smelled of leather and fresh hay. A cot stood along one wall, and sunlight streamed through a dusty window. She wondered whether Morgan slept there. A book lying on the bed caught her eye. Curious, she picked it up.

Collected Poems of the World's Great Poets. The title surprised her. Wildflowers were being used as bookmarks. She opened to one and saw a poem by Edna St. Vincent Millay. She turned to another and read Emily Dickinson's name. Quickly she scanned the other marked sections and saw that every poet she had mentioned on the trail that night to Morgan had been flagged with a flower.

The corner of a page in Elizabeth Barrett Browning's section had been folded over, the last few lines of the poem underlined and circled. Meg read the final, familiar words of "How Do I Love Thee" under her breath.

"... —*I love thee with the breath,*
Smiles, tears, of all my life! — and, if God choose,
I shall but love thee better after death."

A warm flush crept over Meg's body. Had Morgan loved the girl he'd mentioned this way? With his heart and soul? And if he had, where was she now? What had happened to their relationship?

She heard Cammie flush the toilet, hurriedly tucked the dried flower back in place, and dropped the book on the bed. When Cammie emerged, Meg scooted her back outside. Morgan was patiently holding the reins of two horses. He helped Cammie mount, then turned to Meg.

"Need a hand up?"

"Not if he'll stand still."

"Just don't spook him."

"I have no plans to." Meg hoisted her foot into the stirrup and grabbed the saddle horn. At that moment, a fly nipped at the horse's flank and the horse swished its long tail and shifted. Meg gave a little shriek and fell backward. Morgan caught her.

Embarrassed, she struggled to regain her balance. The girls giggled, and the horse gave her a bored look. Morgan's strong arms righted her. "You okay?" His eyes danced with laughter.

"He moved," Meg said weakly, knowing her face was beet red.

"I'll hold him this time."

Meg regained her composure and tried again. Once she was atop the horse, Morgan handed the reins up to her. When their fingers brushed, she felt something akin to an electric shock shoot through her.

"Have a good ride," he said, locking gazes with her.

Her insides turned to mush.

"If we're not back in an hour, come get us."

"Oh, I will," Morgan said, his bright blue eyes not leaving hers. "I surely will, Megan."

SIX

After a week and a half of camp, Katie was feeling confident. No disasters had happened in her cabin, her girls were having fun. And even the reclusive Sarah was coming out of her shell, participating in activities and opening up to her fellow campers. Katie was interested especially in the friendship beginning to grow between Sarah and Dullas—it was good to see Sarah laughing and having fun, although any improvement in her condition was not obvious from her appearance. She had yet to gain any weight, and Katie was worried that the little weight she had put on seemed to be slipping away from her. Still, she was a small girl, and she was only just beginning to settle into life at Jenny House. Katie would continue to keep an eye on her but remained hopeful.

At the moment, Katie's charges were in the rec

center busy with a craft activity, and it was her turn to sort the mail into the proper slots for the campers and staff to pick up later.

She hummed as she worked. It seemed as if everyone had received mail that day. She saw a letter for Lacey with Jeff's return address in the corner. "This should make you happy, girl," she said aloud, and filed it in Lacey's box. The next letter stopped her cold, however. It was addressed to Josh in a distinctly feminine handwriting.

Her heart thudded and jealousy pricked at her insides. Covertly she read the name in the upper left-hand corner: Natalie Brooks. She knew no one named Natalie. Her fingers itched to tear it open and read it.

"Stop it!" she told herself aloud.

"Stop what?"

Katie jumped and whirled. "Dullas!" she barked. "Don't come sneaking up on me like that."

"I wasn't sneaking. I wanted to ask you something."

Katie forced herself to calm down as she shoved the letter into Josh's box. "What? And why aren't you at crafts?"

"I hate crafts. It's dorky and dumb to sit and make pot holders."

"Everybody else is doing it."

Dullas just looked bored. She crossed her arms. "I want to talk to you about Sarah."

"Listen, Sarah's had that bunk for over a week now, so stop badgering me about it."

"It's not about the bunk. It's something else I found out about her."

Curious, Katie asked, "What about her?" Dullas rarely thought of anybody except herself.

"She's adopted. Just like me."

"How do you know that? Did she tell you?"

"I accidentally saw her records."

As the implication of Dullas's confession sank in, Katie caught her breath. "You *read* her file? Good grief, Dullas, you can't go peeking into anybody's records. What were you thinking? It's illegal."

Dullas sniffed, not the least put out by Katie's reprimand. "It was an accident, I told you. I was in Kimbra's office and saw Sarah's file and accidentally knocked it on the floor, and when I picked it up, I just happened to read some stuff."

Katie could imagine how the file had "accidentally" hit the floor. "Well, what if she *is* adopted? It's none of your business."

"But don't you see? Me and Sarah are alike. We both have had cancer and we've both been adopted."

Katie started to tell Dullas that she and Sarah

weren't anything alike, but Dullas looked so impassioned, she held her tongue. "So what's your point?"

"Well, from now on, I'm going to be her special friend."

"Does she want a special friend?"

"You've never been adopted, Katie. You don't know what it's like to always wonder who your real parents are and why they dumped you." Dullas sounded serious.

Katie was pricked by her confession. "You're right, Dullas, I don't know what it's like. Both my parents love me very much. But I met Sarah's adopted parents and her brother and sister. They acted as if they love her very much. When it was time to go, her little brother cried like he was losing his dearest friend. Besides, Kimbra cares about you. So what does it matter who your real parents are? Parents are people who hang around and take care of you and love you."

Dullas nodded. "Sure, that's true, but still a person wonders. You wonder where your real parents are, what they're doing, if they ever think about you. I know my old man's in jail, but my mom, what about her? Where is she? And you wonder if you have grandmas and grandpas, or other brothers and sisters. You wonder a lot of things."

Katie felt the emotional impact of Dullas's words. Of course a person would wonder. It was natural to want to know about your family, your roots. "You may be right," she said slowly. "But don't go making too many assumptions about Sarah. Maybe she doesn't think about it much at all. Maybe she's dealt with her feelings and moved on."

"No one moves on, Katie. You always think about it, and I know Sarah does too."

Katie couldn't dispute what Dullas was saying, so she tried a different tack. "Just remember, if somebody wants you to know something about them, they'll tell you. And that includes Sarah. So my advice to you is, MYOB."

"You're one to talk. Don't you want to know who the girl is that's writing to Josh?"

Dullas didn't wait for Katie's answer. She grinned impishly and skittered away.

Meg sat on a blanket by the lake watching her girls swim and splash. Katie, Lacey, Chelsea, and all their girls were playing keep-away with a giant beach ball. Meg was glad she could sit and watch and didn't have to go into the water. Actually, she was glad she didn't have to be in her bathing suit. She'd tried it on, and even though it was actually a little looser than she remembered, she still hadn't wanted to venture out in it. Especially if there was a chance that Morgan might see her.

"Why aren't you swimming?"

Eric plopped down beside her on the blanket.

"Oh . . . I just didn't feel up to it," she answered.

He studied her for a moment, then grinned. "Oh, it's that girl thing, huh?"

She gave him a blank stare, then reddened. He thought she was having her period. How embarrassing. "Can't a person just not want to go into the water?"

He leaned back on his elbows and offered her a lazy smile. "You're cute when you're mad."

"I'm not mad." Why was she having this conversation? It was so junior high school, and she was almost a college sophomore!

"All right, you're not mad and you're not swimming. What are you doing?"

"Reading."

He made a face. "Don't you get enough of that in school? I sure do."

"I love to read." She gave him a sidelong glance. "Especially poetry."

"Roses are red, violets are blue—" he began.

She interrupted. "Real poetry."

He looked thoughtful, then said, "I think Megan's cute, don't you?" He flashed her another grin. "That's poetry."

She had to laugh. Eric's style *was* disarming. "Do you always charm your way into people's lives?"

"Naw, sometimes I barge right in uninvited." He gazed at her with half-closed eyes, as if sizing her up. "I've been thinking, why don't you and I go for a moonlight ride in one of the canoes some night?"

Canoeing was the alternate activity for the campers who couldn't go swimming for various medical reasons. Meg had paddled a girl around the lake in a canoe just the day before. Still, Eric's offer caught her off guard. "You want to take *me*?"

"Yes, you. What's so strange about that?"

"Nothing, I guess."

"Then you'll go?"

"Um—sure."

He sat straight up. "Terrific. So how about tomorrow night?"

She ran through her obligations mentally. She was supposed to take her girls to Lacey's cabin for board games, but she was certain Lacey could handle twelve girls on her own. "All right," she told Eric. "Tomorrow will be fine if it's all right with Lacey."

"Cool. Why don't I meet you down here about eight-thirty? I'll have the canoe ready to go."

"You're sure you won't tip the canoe over and drown me, now?" she joked.

"Not in my game plan," he said with a wink. "I like to think I'm not that klutzy." He sprang to his feet. "Got to run right now. Almost snack time for the hordes."

Meg watched him lope away, feeling pretty good about herself. It had been easy to say yes to Eric. Why couldn't she be that way with Morgan? What was it about him that made her heart beat faster and her tongue tie in knots whenever she was around him? It didn't make sense to her.

Chelsea dropped to her knees on the blanket and began to towel dry her hair. "I saw you talking to Eric."

"He just came over to say hi."

Chelsea sighed and sat back on her haunches. "I'd give anything if he'd stop long enough to say hi to me."

Meg started. "You would?"

"I think he's so cute."

Meg just nodded. She thought it best not to mention her upcoming canoe ride with him. She knew what it felt like to long for somebody to notice you and never to have him even so much as look your way. It hurt, and she wouldn't hurt Chelsea's feelings for anything in the world. Certainly not for Eric Lawrence. He was nice to her, but he didn't make her pulse flutter and her heart beat faster. No way.

SEVEN

eg met Eric on the shore of the lake the next
evening. In the failing light, the water was
the color of pale emeralds and smooth as silk. A
canoe had been pulled up out of the water onto the
damp ground.

"You made it," he said, looking pleased.

"No problems at all," she said. "I told Lacey I'd
do double duty for her whenever she wanted it."
When Meg had asked Lacey if she could step out for
the evening, Lacey hadn't peppered her with questions. It was understood that counselors needed
some "alone" time because of the intensity of their
job.

"Your yacht awaits," Eric joked, shoving the canoe into the water and helping her into her seat.
Meg looked at Eric's broad shoulders as they started
paddling across the smooth lake.

A whippoorwill called out, and two snow-white herons lifted gracefully off the bank when the canoe glided near. Tree branches dipped low over the water, brushing the surface with lazy, leafy fingers. Tree frogs began their evening symphonies, fireflies dotted the shoreline, and overhead, stars winked on.

"It certainly is peaceful out here." Meg spoke quietly so as not to shatter the silence.

"Better than church," Eric answered over his shoulder.

Meg found the lapping sound their paddles made comforting, and the pull on her arms as the paddle sliced through the water was invigorating.

Since he was in front, Eric guided the canoe with his paddle, and soon Meg realized that he had a destination in mind. "Are we going somewhere in particular?" she asked.

"Yes, straight toward that rock that's jutting out."

She could see it in the gathering twilight and helped him paddle toward it. Beside the rock, Eric swung the canoe around and nudged it close to the reedy shore. He helped her out, pushed the canoe farther into the reeds, and said, "Follow me."

"Where are we going?" she asked. He certainly appeared to have a plan.

"It's a surprise."

"It's getting dark, hard to see."

"Faithful scout have fake fire," he said, flipping out a small high-beam flashlight from his pocket and taking her hand.

She followed him through the woods. The trail widened, then opened out into a meadow ringed by tall trees. In the center of the clearing a blanket had been spread out, and on the blanket were a picnic basket, a couple of pillows, and about half a dozen unlit candles.

"Let me get these going," he said, dropping down on the blanket and taking out a lighter. In seconds, the candles flickered, throwing off warm golden light that sank into darkness beyond the edge of the blanket.

She sat beside him, amazed. "You did all this for me?"

"For us," he said. "I stumbled across this place one day when I went exploring and thought it would be the perfect spot for a moonlight picnic. All I needed was the perfect girl to share it with."

"Why, Eric, this is just beautiful."

"Don't sound so shocked. Guys know how to be romantic when they put their minds to it." He opened the basket and brought out paper plates and a cluster of grapes. "I've got cheese too. And sodas. Lie back. Make yourself comfortable."

Meg fluffed a pillow and stretched out. Above her

a thousand stars twinkled down. All she could think about was how sweet it had been of him to think up the idea. True, his presence didn't make her heart pound the way Morgan's did, but Eric certainly was fun to be with. He had style and imagination. "So, confess, how many girls have you done this with before me?"

"I'm crushed," he said popping a grape into his mouth. "This was carefully premeditated with you in mind."

She nibbled on a slice of cheese. "Well, I'm totally impressed. Thank you. But why me? Why not ask one of the other girls?" She was thinking about Chelsea.

"Because I like you best?" He offered his explanation as a question.

"Lacey's prettier."

Eric shivered. "Cold as ice, that one. Besides, she's got a boyfriend. Ditto Katie. I mean, who wants to run afoul of Josh? He's nuts about that girl and would probably pound my brains in if I so much as looked at her."

"And Chelsea?"

"She's cute, but I'm not interested."

Meg felt let down on her friend's behalf.

"No, I like you best, Megan Charnell, so stop trying to pass me off to some other girl. You're the one I want to be with. End of story." He stretched out beside her, lacing his fingers through hers.

She was flattered that he liked her but not quite sure how she felt about his attention. She wasn't prepared for a summer romance. "What do you do when you're not cooking at camp and taking girls on moonlit picnics?" she asked. "College? A full-time job?"

"I'm starting junior college in the fall. My sister's idea. I live with her and she thinks I need a good education, so to keep the peace, I'm going."

Since she loved college and learning, his answer surprised her. "Don't you have any dreams? Anything you want to do with your life?"

"Make a lot of money."

"That takes a skill."

He rolled over, boosted himself up on his elbows, and peered down at her face. "I can get that lecture from my sister."

"I didn't mean it the way it must have sounded. I was just making conversation." In the candlelight flickering on the side of his face, Meg could appreciate how attractive he was.

"I'd rather go light on the conversation and . . ." He let the sentence trail off.

"And what?" Her pulse began to pound.

"I'd like to kiss you," he said. "Can I?"

No boy had kissed her since Donovan, and she felt woefully out of practice. "Permission granted," she told Eric.

He slid his arm beneath her shoulders and cradled her close. He touched her temple with his lips, sending small shivers down her spine. He kissed her softly on the forehead, then on the cheeks, and then fully on the mouth. The incredible sweetness of it all went through her like melting candle wax.

She let him trail kisses down her neck, along her throat, then back to her mouth. She reveled in the sheer physical pleasure of the moment. When he pulled back, she didn't even open her eyes. She was floating on a sea of warmth, and she savored it the way a hungry person savors a succulent dollop of deep, rich chocolate.

"You taste good," he whispered. "I really like you, Meg."

She couldn't answer. Although she'd experienced physical pleasure in his arms, a part of her felt disengaged and uninvolved. And some voice inside her was saying that he had done this before, and that it worked for him. He knew how to romance a girl, all right. He knew just what to do, just what buttons to push. She was certain that many girls had fallen for his charm, enjoyed his kisses.

"Your picnic was wonderful," she said in his ear.

"Thank you. But I really have to be getting back. You know we're always on call around here, and I shouldn't leave Lacey alone with my group all evening."

Eric's expression turned to one of astonishment, but he recovered quickly. "Are you sure? It's not *that* late. We've only been gone a little while."

"Sorry," she said with her sweetest smile.

If he was mad, he didn't show it. He began to put things away. She helped him blow out the candles, pack up the basket, and fold the blanket.

"You okay?" he asked before they started back to the canoe.

"I'm fine, Eric. Better than I've been in months."

He grinned. "Then we can do this again?"

She shook her head. "Probably not."

"I don't get it."

"I'm not sure I do either, but this is the way it has to be."

They returned to the canoe, got in, and paddled in silence back to the place they'd shoved off from. Once on land, Meg caught his hand. "Thank you, Eric. I really mean that."

"Um—yeah, sure," he said, but he looked totally confused in the pale light of the half moon.

Meg stood on tiptoe and kissed him lightly on the mouth. Then she turned and hurried back toward her cabin, leaving Eric standing on the shore, shaking his head.

In nearby shadows, Morgan stood watching. So Eric had made a move and Meg had gone for it. Morgan felt an edgy spark of jealousy, an emotion he hadn't felt since before Anne died. *It's a free world,* he told himself. *She can do anything she wants, be with anybody she wants.* Still, his insides simmered.

There was nothing he could do about it, except maybe give Eric a wide berth for the next month. The guy got on his nerves. Morgan recalled the moves he himself had once put on Anne and how she'd turned him away. At the time, he'd been hurt. Then he'd learned of her HIV status, and he had been grateful. Anne had been a wonderful girl. He missed her.

Meg was the first girl to interest him since Anne, and she was attracted to a guy like Eric. "Figures," Morgan said under his breath. Life just didn't seem to have a way of working out for him. No, it surely didn't.

EIGHT

Two nights later Morgan was sitting in the tack room rubbing saddle soap into a saddle thrown over a sawhorse when Josh strolled in.

"Would you mind a little company?" Josh asked.

"I thought there was some big movie everybody was watching tonight in the rec center," Morgan answered. He wasn't crazy about having company right then.

"I can't get into it." Josh lowered himself in an old chair. "They won't miss me. I just needed some fresh air. I saw your light on and I knew you weren't at the movie."

"Movies bore me," Morgan said, flipping the saddle around on the sawhorse so he could reach the other side.

"How do you like working at the camp so far?"

"The scenery's pretty, but I miss the wide-open spaces of Colorado."

"I'd like to go out there sometime. From the pictures I see, the place looks awesome."

Morgan worked a few minutes in silence, then asked, "You the only one not at the movie?"

Josh gave him a blank look. "I think so. Why do you ask?"

"Just wondering." Morgan was bombarded with images of Eric sitting in the dark next to Meg, or slipping out with her much as Josh had done so they could be alone.

More silence. Josh broke it with, "You don't like hanging around with us counselors much, do you?"

"I like some of you more than others."

"Who don't you like?"

"Eric sort of gets under my skin."

"Eric's all right. He's kind of a party guy, but he means no harm. Just has some growing up to do."

Morgan grunted.

"What about the rest of us?"

"I've always liked horses better than people. They don't talk much."

Josh burst out laughing. "They don't talk at all."

Morgan grinned in spite of himself, dropped the

polishing rag, and dragged a chair over to face Josh. "Look, I know it seems to all of you that I don't mix. But keeping to myself is just a habit. Back home, I spend lots of time alone out on the trail. It's easy to forget how to talk and socialize. Nothing personal."

In truth, Morgan liked Josh. The guy had a good head on his shoulders and seemed mature in ways the others didn't.

"No offense taken," Josh said.

"You're sweet on Katie, aren't you?" Now that the ice was broken, Morgan felt like talking.

"You could say that. I love her."

"That's hard to tell from a distance."

"Well, things between us are a little one-sided right now." Josh leaned forward, resting his elbows on his knees. "I'd change it in a heartbeat if I could."

"What did you do to back her off?"

"Nothing. She's just confused about her life these days . . . doesn't know exactly what she wants. Her friend Lacey tells me to just be patient. That Katie'll come to her senses soon. That I've got to give her plenty of space until it dawns on her that she loves me too."

"You believe Lacey?"

"I'm willing to wait, I know that much. I think

love is worth the wait. I know Katie's worth the wait."

Morgan was intrigued. He'd never heard a guy talk so openly about his feelings. He had sometimes tried to *show* a girl how he felt, but saying a bunch of sappy words wasn't his way. Maybe that was why he was reading the poetry book. So that he could feel more at ease with pretty words of love.

"You have a brother, Morgan? A big family?"

Morgan shook his head, feeling the old squeeze on his heart when he remembered what fate might await him within his family.

"I had a brother once," Josh said. "He practically raised me because our parents were drowning inside booze bottles. I never told Aaron I loved him. The last day I saw him alive, he came into our grandfather's kitchen and told me to clean up my room. I had my face buried in a cereal bowl and didn't even take the time to look up at him. I just resented him telling me what to do.

"That very day, he walked out onto a football field for practice and had an aneurysm go off in his brain and died. Just like that. I would give anything in this world if I could look up and see him come through the door one more time."

Morgan swallowed. Josh's story touched him, but he didn't know how to respond.

Josh offered a wry smile. "I guess that's why I try my best these days to tell people just what I think. You never know when they walk out of a room if it's going to be the last time you ever see them. That's why I work this camp. Because I know some of these kids won't be around next year. And I want to be sure they have the time of their life while they're here.

"And as long as I'm being brutally honest, I came so I could be around Katie. Because I love her. Whether she loves me or not, I still love her."

Morgan cleared his throat self-consciously. "I hope Katie comes to her senses real soon. A guy can't wait forever."

Josh shrugged. "It sure seems like I've already waited forever. We've been apart for about a year now."

"And you don't date anybody else?"

"Oh, I see a girl named Natalie once in a while. But she knows how I feel about Katie. There's nothing between her and me except friendship." Josh stood and stretched. "I guess I've kept you from your work long enough. And I'm sure that flick's about over by now."

Morgan stood too. "I'm glad you stopped by, Josh," he said, and meant it.

"And I'm glad you didn't mind me talking your ear off. Sorry if I kept you from your chores."

"I can clean saddles anytime," Morgan admitted. "Thanks for talking."

"Thanks for listening." Josh waved and stepped out into the night.

Morgan walked down the row of stalls, and the horses stuck their heads out over the half doors. He stopped in front of the roan mare and scratched behind her ears. "How you doing, old girl?"

The horse nuzzled his pocket, sniffing for a treat. He sometimes carried chunks of carrots. "Nothing tonight," he said.

He couldn't get Josh's words out of his head. Morgan realized that what he'd felt for Anne had been love too. And he couldn't remember telling her. She had died without hearing those words come out of his mouth, and he should have said them.

Megan's face floated into his mind. She was like Anne: sweet, bookish, a little naive. Maybe that was what attracted him to her. She was different. Of course, she would never know how he felt if he never so much as spoke to her. And a snake like Eric could walk away with a treasure he would never really appreciate.

"Might not ought to let that happen," Morgan said absently to the mare.

She didn't answer.

"Did you see Josh slip out of the movie?" Lacey and Katie were walking back to their cabins. Their girls followed them, swinging flashlights so that beams of light bounced off the ground and trees, and talking excitedly among themselves.

"Never noticed," Katie lied.

"He probably went to his cabin to write Natalie a nice long love letter," Lacey said lazily.

"I wish I'd never told you about that letter." Katie was cross. How mean of Lacey to throw the letter up to her. Katie had been unable to keep her mind on the movie because she'd kept waiting for Josh to sneak back inside. But the final credits were rolling across the screen before he did, and she'd been left to wonder where he'd spent the evening. After the lights had come up, everyone had eaten cookies and milk, then headed to the cabins to sleep.

"Maybe I'll write Jeff a nice long sexy letter before I turn out the lights tonight," Lacey mused.

"Lacey," Katie warned. "Cut it out."

Lacey hooked her arm through Katie's. "Oh, don't go getting all angry. I'm just trying to show you the error of your ways."

"You're impossible."

"No, *you're* impossible. I don't know what it's going to take to get the two of you back together again."

"It's not so simple, Lacey. I have a life. A track scholarship. I have three years of college left."

"What? Credits can't transfer? You can't run for the University of Michigan? Give me a break, girl."

Katie sighed. She would be wasting her breath trying to explain to Lacey how she felt. Her gratitude toward Josh was no substitute for love. If she settled for the former instead of the latter, she'd be doing them both great harm.

"Let's just drop it," she said. She slid her arm out of Lacey's and hurried on to her cabin alone.

NINE

"Is it ever going to stop raining?" Dullas complained, her nose pressed to the screen door of the cabin.

It had rained for almost three days straight, and Katie was feeling edgy herself. "Take an umbrella and go down to the rec center," she told Dullas.

"They're playing baby games. It's boring."

"Do it," Katie said. She sensed that Dullas really wanted to go but was reluctant to leave the cabin because Sarah was still there, lying on her bunk, reading.

"Oh, all right," Dullas grumbled. She turned. "You want to come, Sarah?"

"No, thanks. I've just got a few more chapters before I finish the book."

Dullas left, and Katie strolled around the cabin, bored.

"You don't have to hang around for my sake," Sarah said. "Go on down to the rec center."

But Katie hesitated. Mr. Holloway had asked the counselors not to allow any camper to spend too much time alone. "That's okay," she said. "I have some letters to write. I haven't written my mom and dad in two weeks. My dad's a sportswriter, so he writes me all the time from his office computer. I feel guilty when I get three letters in a row and I haven't written even one."

Sarah said nothing.

Katie went over to Sarah's bunk and sat on the edge. "Is Dullas pestering you too much? I know she hangs around a lot. Is she getting on your nerves? She doesn't mean any harm, you know. She's just got a strong case of hero worship."

"I can't imagine why. I'm not much of a role model."

Katie didn't dare confess all that Dullas believed she and Sarah had in common, or how she had come by the information. "Well, she does."

"It's true that she follows me around like a puppy," Sarah conceded. "But I can deal with it. I've got a brother and sister, and they make pests of themselves sometimes. Dullas is all right."

"You—um—having an okay time at camp?"

Sarah lowered her book. "Yeah. I didn't think I

would, but I am." She looked thoughtful. "Actually, I'm glad I'm away this summer. It'll give Tina a chance to be king of the hill."

"What do you mean?"

Sarah marked her place with a bookmark and sat up. "Well, I've been sick a lot, and so the family focus has been on me for a long time. That's been kind of hard on Tina. You know, she sort of gets shoved into the background because she's normal."

"I don't have brothers or sisters," Katie said, "so I've never thought about how one person's sickness can affect the rest of a family, but it makes sense that it would."

"My illness has been tough on all of us. When I came out of remission a year ago and needed a bone marrow transplant . . . well, I'm telling you it was a real blow. Everybody got a jolt of reality. Especially me."

Katie shuddered to think what would happen to her and her parents if her heart transplant failed. Not to mention Josh. She knew that, as with all other organ recipients, her body could reject the transplanted heart at any time. There was no statute of limitations on rejections. Katie had already been through one episode of rejection shortly after the transplant surgery. She had no desire to endure that experience again, but she was virtually helpless to stop it. All she could do was make the most of each precious day that this precious gift, her new heart, gave her.

"What do you mean by 'especially' you?" Katie asked.

"The best donor for a bone marrow transplant is a brother or sister."

"And Tina wouldn't give you any bone marrow?"

"She couldn't because we weren't compatible. No one in my family is, because . . ." Sarah took a deep breath. "Because I was adopted."

Katie tried to act surprised by the news.

"Believe me, it came as a real shock to me. I'd never been told. Then I got the check for a hundred thousand dollars."

"Hey, I got money too!" Katie had never actually met anyone else who had received One Last Wish Foundation money. "I spent some of it to take us all to the Transplant Olympic Games out in Los Angeles. I'm a runner, you know."

"I see you go out early in the morning."

"I have to keep in shape. Track is my life." Katie studied Sarah. "So what did you do with your money?"

"I spent it trying to locate my birth mother."

"Did you find her?"

"I found her, but she couldn't help me," Sarah

said sadly. "And she really didn't want me in her life."

Sensing Sarah's pain, Katie quickly said, "But you got the transplant anyway, didn't you?"

"Yes, but from an unrelated donor, so there's a bigger chance of failure."

"Gosh, I sure hope that doesn't happen."

"Me too. But so far, so good. Coming to this camp was my doctor's idea. She thought it would do me good to be around others who've been sick and are surviving."

"Has it been helpful?"

"Yes." Again Sarah looked thoughtful. "I don't get to feel normal very often. Back home, even my good friends treat me like I might either break or blow up in front of them. But here everybody treats everybody else the same. You don't have to bring someone up to speed on cancer and all that goes along with it. People just *know*. You know what I mean?"

Katie nodded. "It's the best part of Jenny House, feeling as if you belong to some special tribe where nobody is set apart because they have medical problems."

"I just wish there were more kids my age," Sarah said with longing.

"There will be next year. Once the new building

is constructed and there's a full staff, there'll be a lot more teens coming. My first year here is when I met Lacey and Chelsea. We'll be friends forever. You should plan to come back."

"Does that mean Dullas will be back too?"

Katie laughed. "You should have seen her last year. We all wanted to drown her at first. She's a new person since Kimbra adopted her."

Sarah's smile turned wistful. "I became a different person when I found out about my adoption. Cancer was hard enough. Then when I found out I wasn't related to anybody in my family . . . well, that was the hardest part of all." She looked up quickly. "Don't get me wrong, I love my family. They'll do anything for me. But still, I don't really belong to them. Not by blood."

"Is that so important as long as they love you?"

"In my case it makes all the difference in the world. Because I have leukemia. And because family blood and bone marrow are what might cure me forever."

By suppertime the rain had ceased and the sun was peeking through cloud banks. In the rec center the noise was deafening; the campers seemed to be all but bouncing off the walls.

"I sure will be glad to get back to a normal schedule tomorrow," Katie told her three friends above the din.

"They need some major exercise," Meg said.

"And I need earplugs," Chelsea added.

Lacey pushed away from the table. "Follow me," she said. "I have an idea."

Katie fell in behind Lacey, along with Meg and Chelsea. Together they marched over to the boys' tables, where Josh and the other male counselor, Kevin, were eating with their kids. Lacey stopped in front of them, crossed her arms, and tapped her toe.

The boys looked up. "Problems?" Josh asked.

"It's come to my attention," Lacey said in a loud voice, "that your cabins are full of a bunch of weenies."

Josh and Kevin exchanged glances. Josh set down his fork. "We're tougher and better than your dinky little girly-girls."

"I think not," Lacey said.

What's Lacey up to? Katie wondered.

"How do you propose we settle this, then?" Josh asked, a sparkle in his eye.

"Well, I think a nice old-fashioned tug-of-war over a big mud pit could go a long way toward proving that girls are superior to boys."

By now a hush had fallen on the room and campers were listening, elbowing each other, and giggling.

Lacey turned toward the girls' tables. "What do you think, ladies? Can we crush them?"

A chorus of "Yes!" went up.

Josh glanced down the table at his boys. "We've been issued a challenge here, guys. Are we going to let a bunch of girls get away with calling us names?"

A roar of "No!" went up.

"Then you'll meet us over a mud hole tomorrow afternoon at three to prove who's the better team?" Lacey asked.

"We'll be there."

"And the losers will serve the winners dinner tomorrow night?"

"Deal."

Lacey held out her hand, and Josh shook it. "Be prepared to eat dirt," she said.

"Won't happen," he countered.

Lacey marched with her friends and all the girl campers straight out of the rec center.

Outside, Katie eyed her suspiciously. "Are you sure you know what you're doing?"

"Sure do. I'm trying to make certain everyone has a good time."

"And a mud pit is your best idea?"

Lacey smiled sweetly. "Love can be a dirty business."

Confounded, Katie stared at her friend. Lacey was definitely up to something. Katie wasn't exactly sure what it was, but knowing Lacey, it would involve Katie. She didn't like it. But there wasn't a thing she could do about it except be a good sport and join in.

TEN

Meg, her friends, and their charges spent the next morning preparing for the big Mud Event. For kids not well enough to participate, banners were made, along with flags, posters, and colorful pom-poms. "For the cheering section," Katie told them. "We're going to need lots of cheering."

"We'll murder them," insisted Dullas, who Meg thought was getting a little more enthusiastic than necessary.

After lunch they all donned bathing suits or T-shirts and shorts and marched to the area behind the rec center, singing "Heigh ho, heigh ho, it's off to make them muddy . . ." It didn't rhyme, but nobody seemed to care.

Eric had taken on the job of creating the mud hole. Meg was impressed to see how seriously he'd taken his job. He'd dug a pit no deeper than a foot but very big around. Then he'd filled it with water and added plenty of dirt. The mixture was the consistency of pea soup and almost ankle deep.

"The object," Lacey announced to her charges, "is not to fall into it."

The boys showed up, as did the entire staff. Even Mr. Holloway came to observe the big contest. A semicircle of chairs had been assembled for the staff and nonparticipants, and Katie passed out the banners they'd made.

"Wish I could do it," one boy said wistfully.

Christy, Eric's sister, sitting beside him, said, "Next year, Marty."

Meg realized that Marty was a cystic fibrosis patient and probably had a respiratory problem that kept him from participating. It touched her because she could tell just how much these kids with terrible medical problems wanted to be like everybody else—they wanted to have fun and do what others their ages did.

"Will you hold my towel for me?" she asked Marty. "I know I'm on the other side, but I'd sure appreciate it."

He beamed at her for his answer.

Morgan stepped up to the side of the pit with a length of rope. A clean white handkerchief was knotted in the rope's center. "This is strong rope," he told both sides. "Strong enough to hold a wild horse, so I know it can't break." He handed one end to the girls' team, the other to the boys'.

"The rules are simple," Eric announced, stepping up and grabbing hold of the handkerchief. "This hanky must pass completely to one side of the pit or the other. Of course, when this happens the bulk of the losing side will be *in* the pit, but you'll pick up on that, I'm positive."

Both teams cheered.

"I have a whistle," Eric said, and blew it to make his point. "Whenever you hear this whistle, you stop pulling because that means the game's over and I'm declaring a winner. Of course, those of you in the mud will probably catch on to that too."

Both teams booed.

"At no time will any of you call the other team names or get the referee—that's me—muddy. Are the rules clear?"

Both sides yelled their approval.

One of the boys on Josh's team shouted, "Hey, there's more of them than there are of us, Josh."

Josh turned. "So what? We can take them. Are we men or mud daubers?"

"Men!" came the resounding reply.

Meg took the lead position on the rope, with Katie right behind her. Lacey positioned herself in the middle, and Chelsea became last in the line. About twenty-five girls sandwiched themselves between the counselors. Meg grinned across the mud pit at Josh, who was lead man on the other team. "Now, don't get me muddy," she called.

"Fat chance," he said. "We may be fewer in number, but we're better."

"Oh, puh-leeze," she said. "Whine, whine, whine."

"Now, wait a minute," Josh said. "If that's your attitude, I think we should sweeten the pot. Just between us counselors, that is."

"How so?"

He looked thoughtful. "I know. Losers have to clean the winners' cabins, do their laundry, and serenade them outside their cabin windows for two nights in a row."

Meg glanced over her shoulder and caught Katie's and Lacey's eyes. "What do you think?"

"I think it'll be fun having Josh and Kevin make our beds," Katie answered.

"Fat chance," Kevin yelled.

Meg turned to her line of girls. "This is for our dignity, ladies. Let's make it count!"

The group responded with a cheer.

Eric stepped up, grabbed the handkerchief and

held the now slack rope high for all to see. Meg dug in her heels. She felt Katie tense behind her. Eric put the whistle in his mouth. He gave a blast and dropped the handkerchief, and immediately the rope went taut.

Meg felt her feet sliding toward the edge of the mud pit. "They're stronger than I thought," she said through gritted teeth.

"Pull!" Lacey yelled from behind.

On the sidelines, the others erupted with yelps, catcalls, and chants of encouragement. From the corner of her eye, Meg could see Eric, crouching down, watching the white handkerchief intently.

"Go! Go! Go!" someone shouted.

The handkerchief edged toward the girls. Seconds later it inched toward the boys. From behind her, Meg heard Dullas utter a swear word and heard Lacey say, "Save it, Dullas. Pull!"

Meg hung on for all she was worth until her sneakers began to skid ever closer to the edge of the pit. "Help!"

"Don't let go!" Kimbra yelled from the sidelines. "You can do it."

Meg pulled hard, watching Josh slide ever closer to the edge of disaster. *A . . . few . . . more . . . tugs,* she told herself. By now her legs felt as if they were on fire and her back muscles were screaming for mercy. Her hands ached from holding the thick rope.

"Whose bright idea was this, anyway?" Katie gasped over Meg's shoulder.

"Lacey's," Meg grunted.

"Remind me to kill her."

"Me first."

All at once the rope went slack and the line of girls fell backward. Instantly the rope went tight again, but Meg, completely off balance, could do nothing to stop her forward momentum. She tumbled face first into the mud. Seconds later half the line toppled in with her. She came up sputtering, to the blast of the whistle and Eric shouting, "The winners and champions, the boys' team!"

A cheer went up, but Lacey rose out of the mud and shouted, "You cheated!"

"Did not," Josh said with a laugh. "We just used strategy to defeat your superior numbers. We threw you off balance; gravity did the rest."

"Are we going to take this, ladies?"

A shout of "No!" and surge of bodies brought Josh and most of his team into the mucky mire. Soon mud was flying everywhere and staff and side-liners alike were ducking.

Eric blasted the whistle, but someone yelled, "Get him!" and moments later he too was flung into the mud.

"Don't touch the ref!" he kept shouting. "Remember the rules!" But his shouts were lost in shrieks of laughter as he disappeared in a tangle of muddy arms and legs.

Every time Meg tried to crawl to the edge of the pit, she slipped and skidded back into the mud. She was so weak from laughing and slinging mud at everyone, she could scarcely catch her breath.

By the time the staff broke out the hoses and began rinsing kids off, Meg was resigned to sitting in the middle of the pit to await her turn. Richard Holloway announced, "To the lake!" and kids took off running. Meg, her friends, and a few stragglers were left behind in the muddy hole.

Lacey, covered from head to toe in dark brown gunk, said, "I've always wondered what I'd look like as a brunette. Anybody got a mirror?"

Katie, equally slathered with mire, said, "The worst part is now we have to do their laundry."

"We got ripped off," Chelsea said. Because she'd been the last in line, she wasn't as caked with mud as the others. "I think we should be let off the hook."

"I still think they cheated," Lacey said in a huff.

"Face it," Katie said, "they outsmarted us. We've got to pay up."

Meg agreed and wiped slop from her mouth. "Ugh, this stuff tastes awful. Let's get out of here."

Suddenly a hand reached down. Meg looked up, shading her eyes from the bright, hot sun. Morgan stood over her.

"Want some help?" he said in his lazy drawl.

ELEVEN

"I'm really dirty," Meg said, feeling self-conscious. Morgan chuckled. "I can see that."

She felt Katie nudge her from behind, so she held out her mud-caked hand and let Morgan guide her out of the pit. He walked with her to the edge of the woods.

"Don't mind us," Lacey called. "We'll get out on our own."

"Hush!" Meg heard Katie say.

Ignoring her friends, Meg said, "Well, you can't ever say you haven't seen me at my worst." Her chest felt tight, and she knew it was because she was standing so close to Morgan. She tried to scrape some of the mud off her face.

"Let me," he said, holding out a towel. He gently wiped her cheeks, forehead, and neck. "What do you know, there's a girl under all that gunk."

"I'll never get clean again," she said, taking the towel and wiping her arms and hands. By now the towel was sopping and a hideous brown color. She could only imagine what she must look like. "Thanks."

His eyes danced with amusement. "You all were good sports, and the kids had a blast. It was fun to watch."

"Yeah, how come you're so clean and neat?"

His denim shirt was only lightly spotted with mud, and she was positive it had come from her.

"I decided not to give the guys an unfair advantage, what with my superior strength and all."

"Oh, you," she chided. "You just didn't want to get muddy."

"You're right about that." He laughed. "Let me walk you down to the lake so you can rinse off."

She took a step. "Yuck. I've got mud oozing between my toes. Feels awful."

He walked with her. In spite of her sticky condition, she felt light and happy. Just being around Morgan lifted her spirits. "You know," she said, "there are people who pay hundreds of dollars to soak in mud so they can be beautiful. They must be crazy."

When they got to the lake, she saw the campers jumping and splashing in the water. "Come this way," Morgan said. He led her to a more isolated area. "Go on in and wash off. I'll wait here on the bank."

Meg walked out into the water shyly, knowing he was watching her. *Please don't let me fall in a deep hole,* she begged silently. That was all she needed, to make even more of a fool of herself in front of him. She was sure his onetime girlfriend had been poised and ladylike, not at all like her. Odds were *she* didn't go rolling around in a mud pit.

Meg rubbed at her arms and legs, and the water swirling around her turned a dirty shade of dark brown. She held her breath and went under the surface, trying to cleanse her hair of the clinging mud. She came up and rubbed her arms again, but no matter how hard she scrubbed, her skin remained a pale brown. Finally she gave up and staggered back to shore, the water pouring off her. Her sneakers squeaked across the grass.

"Sit with me a minute," Morgan invited her.

She dropped beside him in a wet heap. "I feel better," she said, "but something tells me I've got a long way to go before I reach clean."

"You look fine to me. I like a girl who isn't too prissy, who doesn't mind getting a little mussed up. On my aunt and uncle's ranch, we get city dudes all the time trying to catch a piece of the Old West.

They buy all these fancy clothes—as if a horse cares what you look like—and within days these same people are wearing faded jeans and the most comfortable shirts they can find. Ranch life isn't for the fashion-conscious."

Meg laughed. "My dad's a surgeon, so mostly he wears scrubs all day. In medicine you'd better like green because that's the color you're wearing most of the time."

They sat in a comfortable silence, looking out over the lake. A heron, wading along the shore, darted its long beak under the water and came up with a small fish, which it quickly devoured. The sound of the campers' laughter started to fade, and Meg said, "I think everyone's headed back to their cabins to get cleaned up before supper. I'd better go too."

She started to rise. He caught her arm. "Could I ask you a favor?"

Her heart seemed to trip, then go on beating. "Sure."

"I've—uh—been reading a lot of poetry lately. Some of the poets you mentioned to me."

"You have?" She hoped she sounded sufficiently surprised.

"I like them. Some more than others, of course. I was wondering if you'd get together with me and help me understand them. I'd like to really catch on to what they're saying with all those nice words. Would you do that with me, Meg?"

If he'd asked her to walk across the lake on her hands, she would have agreed. "Of course I will. But I'm no expert. I don't always get the point of a poem either."

"You've got to be smarter about it than I am," he said with a grin. "The words are pretty, but the meaning sometimes escapes me."

"I'll sure try to help," she told him.

He helped her to her feet. "I'll walk you home."

Her legs felt rubbery, both from the exertion of the tug-of-war and from Morgan's proximity. "Thanks," she said. "The hot water's probably all used up by now anyway."

"I've got a shower down at the barn."

"That's all right," she said hastily as images of herself in his shower flitted through her head. "I need to get fresh clothes and all. Plus, because of our big mouths, we've got laundry, bedmaking, and serenading to do."

They were at the cabin now, and she saw her girls peering out through the screens and heard them giggling and whispering.

"Can you meet me at the barn tomorrow night after supper?" Morgan asked.

"I'll be there." She walked into the cabin, fairly floating off the ground.

The next morning after breakfast, Katie went to Josh's cabin to keep her part of the tug-of-war bargain. Meg had gone on to Kevin's cabin, and they had agreed that the next morning Chelsea would make Kevin's bed while Lacey made Josh's. Katie entered the cabin cautiously and was relieved to discover that it was empty. The area the boys used looked fairly neat, but the room off to the side where Josh stayed looked as if a bomb had gone off in it.

Shocked by the disarray, Katie grumbled that he'd probably trashed the place on purpose just so she'd have a mess to clean up.

She set to work. Clothes lay in heaps, so she sorted through them, piling the dirty ones in a corner to take with her to the laundry room when she left. She picked up a T-shirt and was struck by the scent of Josh's familiar aftershave that clung to the fabric. Her heart lurched as she remembered nights of being in his arms, the wonderful fragrance enveloping her.

She opened his closet door and fingered the few clothes hanging there. She saw a shirt she'd bought him, now faded from being laundered so many times. She thought of the time they'd been together at the Transplant Games, of the fun they'd had, of his soft kisses in the moonlight.

With a shake of her head she shut the door on the closet and on the memories.

She went to his bed and was dismayed at the snarl he'd made of his sheets. She threw everything off the bed, then remade it, making sure the corners were tucked in neatly and the top blanket folded properly. She picked up his pillow and found stray hairs. She hugged the pillow and buried her face in it, recalling all the times she'd snuggled against his broad chest, listening to the beat of his heart while he smoothed her hair and whispered, "I love you, Katie."

She jerked herself into the present, fluffed the pillow and tossed it on the bed, then turned her attention to his dresser. A photo caught her eye, and she picked it up. It was of Josh and a smiling girl with long, dark hair. They had their arms around each other, and it was obvious they were at a party. Across the bottom, a feminine hand had written: *To the good times! Love, Natalie.*

Katie's heart thudded and her throat constricted. So this was his new girlfriend. She was pretty. It didn't take a rocket scientist to figure out why Josh liked her. Confronted by the image of the girl, Katie felt the sting of jealousy.

She was scrutinizing the photo so hard that she didn't hear the footsteps behind her and had no idea that she was no longer alone until she heard Josh's deep voice ask, "Can I help you, Katie?"

TWELVE

Katie dropped the photo as if it were on fire. She spun around. "I—I didn't know you were here. I thought I was alone."

"I just came back for Andy's catcher's mitt. We're getting up a game of baseball."

She absolutely hated being caught snooping. And Josh had caught her red-handed. She held her head high in an attempt to restore her dignity. "I've made your bed and cleaned up a little. The place was a mess."

"I'm a messy guy. You know that."

Back home, when they had dated and she'd gone to visit him at his grandfather's, his room had often been less than orderly. She'd joked with him about it and he'd told her, "What I need is a girlfriend who loves junking up a place as much as I do." She wondered if Natalie was that kind of girl.

"Well, it's none of my business," she said with a shrug, and started past him toward the heap of dirty clothes.

He stepped around her and up to his dresser. "What do you think of Natalie?" he asked.

Katie's cheeks felt hot. "I hardly got a look at her."

"She's a nice girl. You'd like her."

Katie doubted that. "Maybe I can meet her sometime."

"Maybe." He set down the photo. "Katie, I hope that when we get back home we can be friends again."

"We are friends. Aren't we?"

"You've gone out of your way to ignore me. That's not how friends treat friends." He sounded hurt.

Ashamed, Katie shrugged. "It's nothing personal, Josh. I'm just giving us both lots of space."

"If we had any more space between us, I'd be on the moon."

She couldn't help smiling. "This summer has really been great so far," she said. "I like being here. I like having you here."

"You do?"

"Yes, Josh. It's nice to look up and see you every day. Like old times."

He flashed her a smile that almost made her heart melt. "Thanks for telling me that. It helps."

"Helps?"

"Helps me believe that we aren't a hopeless case."

She smiled shyly. "Nothing's hopeless." She bent and picked up his heap of clothes. "Except maybe your laundry. It looks pretty grim."

"Thanks for doing it."

"You beat us. I owe you, remember?"

"Well, we did sort of trick you."

"I know, but we'll get over it."

She eased out the door, clutching the clothes, and the last sound she heard as she walked toward the laundry room was Josh whistling.

That night at supper in the rec hall, Katie sat with her friends, picking at her Jell-O. "What's the matter?" Lacey asked.

"Nothing."

Lacey leaned over to the others. "Which is shorthand for 'Lots, but I'm not going to tell you-all.' "

"Can't a person have a personal thought around here?" Katie asked.

"Sounds like a Josh encounter to me," Lacey said with authority as she leaned back in her chair.

Katie was starting to snap, "No, it wasn't," when the rec doors opened and Josh, Kevin, and Eric strolled in. They wore makeshift Mexican-style out-fits—big, cheap *sombreros* and horse blankets thrown around their shoulders. Eric carried a guitar, and the other two held roses in their teeth. They slowly walked over to where the girls sat and bowed from the waist.

"We have come to sing for you," Kevin announced in a terrible Spanish accent.

"I thought we were supposed to sing for you," Katie said. The three boys looked so ridiculous that she could hardly keep from laughing aloud.

"We have heard all of you sing," Josh said. "It is not a pretty noise."

"Why, you . . ." Lacey picked up a blob of Jell-O as if to toss it at them, but Chelsea grabbed her hand.

"Methinks the *señorita* is miffed," Eric said. He'd drawn a thin mustache on his upper lip with eyebrow pencil.

Kids were leaving their seats and gathering around the girls' table. "Hey, Josh," one boy called out. "Are those my shower shoes you're wearing?" He was a big kid, heavyset and bald from chemotherapy.

Katie looked at Josh's feet and saw that he wore shower sandals shaped like little boats. She muffled her laughter with her hand.

"We have a song for the pretty girls," Josh said in an equally bad Spanish accent. He glanced at his *compadres.* "The music, Señor Eric."

Eric strummed the guitar, and together the three boys sang "Wind Beneath My Wings." They were not quite on key, but as they went along, they began to sound decent, almost good. And when they sang the refrain, Josh looked straight into Katie's eyes.

She felt the look all the way to her bones.

When the song was over, the campers cheered and stomped. Lacey shook her head, and Chelsea gave Eric a dreamy look. Meg leaned over to Katie and said, "So, do you think they have a shot at singing careers?"

"Probably not," Katie answered, but her insides were still quivering from the expression in Josh's eyes.

The three boys offered dopey grins, handed each girl a rose, and bowed one final time. "However, *señoritas,*" Kevin said, "this was just a demonstration of how proper singing is done."

"Yes," Josh said. "Make certain your song to us is equally well done."

Lacey stuck out her tongue.

The three boys laughed and moved out of the rec center. Campers tagged after them, knocking off their *sombreros* and taking turns wearing them.

"Now, how are we going to follow their act?" Chelsea asked.

Lacey rolled her eyes. "Who wants to?"

"It's our turn tomorrow night to sing to them," Chelsea said. "We've got to do something spectacular."

"Yeah, Lacey," Katie chimed in. "This is all your doing anyway. Think of something."

Lacey sighed. "Oh, all right. I'll come up with some kind of idea. But the three of you had better go along with it."

"Suits me," Meg said with a shrug. "I'd love to inflict terminal embarrassment on the three of them."

"Not Eric," Chelsea said quickly. "I'm sure the other two dragged him into this."

"So we've got a little soft spot for Eric, have we?" Lacey asked.

Chelsea shrugged self-consciously. "I think he's cute. Don't you?"

"He thinks he's cute too," Lacey said.

"That's not kind," Chelsea said.

"Maybe. But it's the truth."

Meg kept quiet, glad she had never told any of them about her canoe adventure with Eric. Ever since that night, they had been polite to each other, but he'd gotten the message that she wasn't interested in a relationship with him and had left her alone.

"Lacey, don't get on Chelsea's case," Katie said. "If she wants to go after Eric, let her."

"Be my guest," Lacey said.

Chelsea looked crestfallen. "He practically ignores me. I have to start the conversation if I even want to have him speak to me."

"Don't give up," Katie said with a kind smile. "Sooner or later he'll realize what a terrific person you are."

Chelsea looked out the window pensively. "Well, it had better be sooner. We're running out of time. Only three more weeks left of camp."

THIRTEEN

Morgan paced in front of the stalls. Maybe she wasn't coming. He wanted Meg to show up more than he'd let on the afternoon of the tug-of-war. He hadn't wanted to sound too pleased when she'd agreed, but maybe he hadn't sounded pleased enough. Maybe he'd been too casual and she thought it didn't matter to him either way. Maybe the idea of discussing poetry with him had turned her off. Maybe—

A horse whinnied, and he looked up to see Meg strolling through the woods toward the stables. He felt tremendous relief.

"Sorry, I'm late," she said with a smile. "But I had to get my girls settled in at Chelsea's cabin. They were real wiggleworms tonight."

"No problem. I was just checking on the horses and getting them bedded down."

She reached up and scratched the roan mare's muzzle. "And to think I was scared of these horses when I first got here. Why, they're as gentle as puppies."

Morgan laughed. "They can be stubborn, but they're a good bunch. Come on. I've fixed up a place for us in the tack room."

He was nervous. What if Meg thought he was overdoing things?

As they walked to the tack room, Meg wiped her sweaty palms on her shorts. She couldn't have felt more agitated. Being in the same place as Morgan made her heart beat faster and her hands tremble. "I'm walking slowly because my legs are killing me," she told him. "And my back too. All that pulling was more physical exertion than I'm used to."

"I have some salve you can borrow," he said. "When I do the rodeo circuit and get thrown by broncos, I get so sore I can hardly move. The salve really helps."

They entered the tack room, and Meg caught her breath. He'd worked hard to fix it up. A small table stood in the center of the room, and he'd borrowed a checked tablecloth from the kitchen. Two candles were burning, and a vase of wildflowers sat between them. The air smelled of old leather and saddle soap but also held a hint of jasmine.

"Very nice," Meg murmured.

Morgan hoped she was sincere. In the warm glow of the candles and the lone lamp hung on the wall, he thought she looked soft and pretty. And she smelled wonderful, of fresh soap and wild grass mingled with gardenias.

Meg sat in one of the chairs. Morgan fetched the salve and gave it to her. "Use it for a couple of days after a good hot shower. Your muscles will feel better. Promise."

"Thanks," she said, tucking the can into her pocket. He sat across from her, and she fingered the book of poetry on the table. She wasn't sure how to begin.

"You got clean, I see," Morgan said with a little laugh.

"It took three hot showers and half a bottle of shampoo."

"Well, you look terrific."

She blushed, cleared her throat, and asked, "Do you have a favorite poet?"

"I keep coming back to Emily Dickinson. There's something special about her stuff. Some of it's sad, but really honest."

Meg opened the book to Dickinson's section. "I know what you mean. Take this one: 'Because I could not stop for Death,/He kindly stopped for me—' "

"Don't!" Morgan blurted out.

Startled, she looked up to see a look of pure pain on his face. "Wh—What's wrong?"

"Not that poem." He shoved his chair back and stood. "It has . . . memories for me."

Meg's heart hammered. Why had she started with *that* one? "Do you want to tell me about it?"

"It was Anne's favorite."

"Is she your girlfriend?" Meg felt a terrible letdown. He was substituting her for this Anne. It was Anne he wanted to be with this evening.

"She . . . She was somebody I cared for a lot. But she died."

"Oh, no, Morgan. I'm so sorry."

"She was special to me." His words were halting, as if he was having trouble getting them out. "I was able to spend the last weeks of her life with her, and I read poetry to her sometimes. She was in a lot of pain, you see, and the poetry soothed her. That poem was a special one to her."

Tears welled in Meg's eyes, for Morgan's loss, for her own loss of Donovan. "I—I had a friend who died too," she said. "He needed a liver transplant, but they couldn't find a donor for him in time. My father was his surgeon. Daddy did everything he could, but nothing could save Donovan."

The intensity of the painful memories shocked her. Meg had thought all that was behind her and that time had dulled her hurt, but it had returned as sharp as a sword to pierce her with new pain.

Morgan crouched in front of her, feeling like a jerk. Why had he poured out his guts about Anne? He'd only reminded Meg of someone she'd lost. A boyfriend? Morgan couldn't guess. "Looks like we both know something about losing," he said. "I didn't mean to bring back bad memories for you."

"They're good memories too," she said, dipping her head so that he wouldn't see the tears brimming in her eyes. "Donovan wanted so much to live. He got cheated."

"Anne wanted to live too. She fought hard. Harder than any wild horse I've ever known. I like to think that death didn't come to take her, but, like the poem says, she went out to his coach and got in of her own free will."

Meg nodded in understanding. "I'm glad I came to help at this camp. Whenever I look at the kids, I see regular kids who want to have fun."

"You're giving them that. You should be proud."

"You are too," she said. "It's the least we can do,

don't you think?—help others out. Donovan is still helping. He made sure there was a special house for families to stay in so they could be with their sick children. Did Anne do anything special like that?"

Morgan was drawn up short. Anne had given him money for his genetic test for Huntington's chorea, but he couldn't tell Meg about that. He stood, pulled Meg to her feet, and turned her face upward so that he could look down into her eyes. "This evening didn't turn out like I planned," he said. "I've made you sad, and for that I'm sorry."

"It's all right." He had subtly shifted the subject. She knew he was through talking about Anne. And himself.

"I think we should call it quits tonight. I'm not in the mood to read any more poetry."

She felt rebuffed, as if he'd walked to the edge of a special place with her, then retreated. Or maybe he just didn't want to be with her. "All right. Maybe some other time."

She told herself to walk away, but she couldn't.

"Come here," he said, and gently tugged her against him.

Meg began to cry then, soft, muffled sobs. She wept, her face buried in his chest, soaking the soft fabric of his shirt with her tears. She wept for all the

kids at the camp, for Morgan and for herself, for
Donovan, and for Anne too. She wept for those
whose lives were no more; for the lost potential of
youth, dreams, and plans; and for the deaths that
medical science, with all its tests, chemicals, and ma-
chines, could not postpone.

"*Pssst*, Meg, wake up!"

Meg struggled out of a sound sleep to open her
eyes and saw Lacey leaning over her bed in the dark.
"Wh—What's wrong?"

"Serenade time," Lacey said.

Meg glanced out her window and saw that it was
still pitch dark. "Are you kidding? What time is it?"

"Four A.M. Hurry up." Lacey sounded impatient.
"Katie and Chelsea are waiting outside."

Meg threw off her covers and fumbled to get
dressed. Regular wake-up time was seven, and she
hadn't slept well once she'd turned off the lights the
night before. She'd kept thinking about Morgan, his
Anne, and Donovan.

The girls slipped outside. Katie was there, holding a flashlight, and Chelsea stood beside her with
another flashlight and two portable CD players. "Is
this a smart thing to do?" Meg asked.

"Look," Lacey told her, "nothing was ever said

about the *time* we had to serenade them. I'm just taking some creative liberty with our bargain."

They crept through the woods to the boys' two cabins and placed a CD player under each counselor's window.

"What music have you picked out?" Katie asked.

"John Philip Sousa marching music," Lacey whispered. "I went through Mr. Holloway's collection. He really has some old-time stuff, but it's perfect for what we need right now."

Chelsea flipped on her flashlight. "I'll turn on the one under Kevin's window. Just flash me a signal so we can do it in unison."

"Once I flash, count to three, then push the Play button. The CDs are all cued and ready."

Meg giggled. Eric slept in the same room as Kevin, so he'd get blasted awake too. This would fix the three *amigos*.

Chelsea stole away and moments later flicked her flashlight. Lacey flashed Katie's light in return.

"One, two, three," Lacey whispered. Then she pushed the Play button and a blare of marching music shattered the stillness.

From inside Josh's room they heard bumps, thuds, shouts, and yelping.

"Good morning!" Lacey yelled.

Josh staggered to his window, rubbing the top of his head.

"Run for it!" Katie shouted. And, grabbing up the CD players, the girls raced toward the safety of their cabins, laughing every step of the way.

FOURTEEN

At breakfast the whole camp was talking about the girls' prank. Josh and his buddies were grumpy, but the kids thought it had been a good trick. "Serenades are over," Katie announced to the entire assembly. "And don't ever tell us we can't make music," she said to Josh and his friends.

The hall applauded, and Katie and her three friends gave each other high fives.

In the afternoon Meg took her girls to their trail riding activity. The afternoon was hot and sticky. Once the ride was over and they had returned to the barn and dismounted, Morgan pulled her aside. "Can you talk a minute?"

"Sure." Just being close to him made her mouth go dry. She sent the girls to the cabin, promising to follow in a few minutes.

When they were alone, Morgan said, "You know what? I'd like to start over with you."

"How so?"

"I made you cry last night, and that's not what I wanted to do."

She shook her head. "You didn't make me cry. It just happened. That's the problem with memories. Sometimes they sneak up on you when you least expect it. I miss Donovan, but I can't bring him back. Knowing him, spending time with him, was good for me. It helped me understand that not everybody has a wonderful, happy life. He helped me see that doing something good and worthwhile in spite of your own problems can make your life count for a whole lot more. It made me want to help others."

Morgan grinned. "I guess that's why I like you, Meg. You see beyond the end of your own nose. A lot of girls don't."

Because she knew that Morgan didn't pass out compliments lightly, a single one from him was worth a hundred from Eric. "That's nice of you to say."

"How'd you like to go on a moonlight trail ride with me tonight?"

"I'd like it very much."

"Then meet me at the barn about eight and we'll go."

She agreed without hesitation and started toward the cabins. She'd ask Lacey to watch her girls tonight. And this time she'd tell Lacey why—because she had a date with Morgan. No use keeping secrets now. Actually, she wanted to shout it out at the top of her lungs. She decided to tell all her friends that night when they were together at supper.

Meg bounded into Lacey's cabin and found Lacey writing; her girls were doing crafts in the rec center. "I owe Jeff a long letter," Lacey said. "He's really good about writing, and I haven't been."

Meg asked Lacey her favor and Lacey agreed, but when Meg turned to leave, Lacey stopped her.

"As long as we're alone," she said, "there is something I want to talk to you about."

"Really? What's that?"

"Sit down." Lacey pulled up a chair next to her bed and offered it to Meg. She looked apprehensive, which wasn't at all like her.

"Is something wrong?" Meg asked.

"I think that's my question to you."

"What do you mean?"

Lacey paced, then sat on the bed across from

Meg. "Listen, I'm not trying to meddle in your business, but we're friends, aren't we?"

"Of course we are."

Lacey took a deep breath. "I don't want you to think I'm out of line in talking to you about this subject. It—It's just that I'm concerned about you."

"About me? Why?"

"I—um—can't help noticing that you've lost a lot of weight since the day camp started. Well, maybe not a lot," Lacey corrected herself, "but you're thinner than you were."

Except for her friend Alana, back home, Meg had not discussed her weight with anyone. How could a tall, slim, pretty girl like Lacey ever appreciate the frustration of a weight problem? "Yeah, I guess I have lost some weight. And frankly, I'm pleased about it. I've sort of struggled with being overweight most of my life. It's nice to be thinner."

"Um—are you doing anything to help it along?"

By now Meg was thoroughly confused. What was Lacey trying to ask her, anyway? "I'm not sure I get your drift, Lacey."

Lacey's brow knitted. "Listen, diabetes can cause weight problems too. I used to be heavier."

"*You* were overweight?" Meg couldn't believe it.

"I *thought* I was overweight. I got carried away and, well . . . I tried bulimia to fix it."

Meg let Lacey's confession sink in. "You forced yourself to throw up?" She'd known a girl at college who was bulimic, and she'd thought it was gross.

"It seemed like a good idea at the time," Lacey said, "except that I really messed up my diabetic control and ended up in the hospital."

"I didn't know."

Lacey shrugged. "It was a really dumb thing to do, and I don't recommend it to anybody."

Meg sat staring at Lacey, realizing she should say something. Then, slowly, the light of revelation broke through. "Are you asking me if I'm bulimic?"

"I'm not being nosey," Lacey said hastily. "It's just that you're my friend, and friends need to look out for friends."

Meg would have laughed if the subject hadn't been so serious. And she knew that it probably hadn't been easy for Lacey to admit such a thing to her. "I'm a doctor's daughter, Lacey," Meg said. "I know too much about certain things. And I know that bulimia isn't a very smart way to control your weight."

"So you're not doing it?" Lacey was like a bulldog in her persistence.

"I'm not doing it," Meg said.

Lacey looked so relieved, she sagged in her chair.

"Good! I'd hate to see you messed up that way. Bulimia almost killed me."

Meg couldn't even feel insulted that Lacey had suspected her of such a thing. For a diabetic, bulimia would be a death warrant. "I know I've lost weight since I've been here." Meg chose her words carefully. "But I'm sure it's because I've been so physically active. I mean, there's no time to sit around snacking like I do at home or at school. I'm practically busy around the clock. And way too tired to eat. But I'm glad I'm losing weight. It's not easy to always feel like the chubby one, or to have to buy clothes a couple of sizes bigger than my friends do."

"Been there, done that," Lacey said. "But when I tightened up on my diet, it was easier to keep the weight off. And you're right, this place does keep you busy."

"The trick is keeping the weight off once I get back to college. I study a lot, and that sometimes leads to nonstop eating," Meg admitted.

"Maybe you should get out more."

"What? And let my grades slide?" Meg feigned horror, and Lacey laughed.

"So, you're not mad at me for poking my nose into your private life?"

Meg shook her head. "I understand where you're coming from."

Lacey leaned over and gave Meg a quick hug. "Good. Then we won't talk about it again." She stood up, glancing at her watch. "Got to run."

She had a look in her eye that Meg had come to recognize as scheming.

"What are you up to, Lacey Duval?"

"Moi?" Lacey pointed to herself innocently, then said, "Don't you remember? It's my turn to make Josh's bed."

"And?"

Lacey flashed an impish grin. "And I'm off to short-sheet him."

Chelsea was late in coming to supper that night, so Meg kept her news about her date with Morgan to herself. Where was that girl, anyway? Meg was so eager to share her news that she thought she'd explode.

She half listened to Katie and Lacey talking together. Golden sunlight spilled through the windows. Soon the long shadows of evening would stretch out, and later the moon would rise and she would go to the barn to meet Morgan. And this time there would be no sad talk. There would be just the two of them together in the moonlight. Her pulse raced at the thought of it.

Meg heard a commotion outside the door, and

through the screen she saw Chelsea running fast. Chelsea burst through the door with a bang, saw the three of them, and ran over.

She skidded to a stop and grabbed the back of a chair. Her face was the color of paste. She cried, "Katie, come quick! Josh has had a terrible riding accident and he's been taken to the hospital!"

FIFTEEN

Katie paced the floor of the hospital's emergency waiting room like a caged cat. She felt cold and numb, and her heart seemed permanently squeezed as if by some giant hand. As soon as Chelsea had made her announcement, Katie and Lacey had raced to Lacey's car and to the hospital. Lacey had driven down the winding country roads at great speed, to the glass and brick building where Josh lay behind the triage doors. The two of them had been there an hour already, but still there was no word on Josh's condition.

Richard Holloway was there too, but he could find nothing out either. Lacey grumbled and complained, but no one came out to enlighten them.

Katie's thoughts alternated between "He's fine" and "He's dead." She felt like a tightly wound spring, or a volcano ready to blow.

She let out a little sob, and Lacey quickly put her arm around her. "He'll be all right. I know he will."

Katie nodded, but she didn't feel reassured.

Morgan showed up, looking grim. "Any news?"

"Nothing," Lacey told him.

"Do you know what happened?" Mr. Holloway asked.

"I've pieced it together by asking some questions," Morgan said. "It seems that Josh got wind that two of his campers had decided to go check out the construction site for themselves."

"But it's off limits," Mr. Holloway said, sounding alarmed.

"Sure it is, but you know how kids can be. As soon as Josh found out what they were doing, he came to the barn and asked for a horse. He figured he could beat them to the site through the woods on horseback."

"He would never let a kid get hurt if he could help it," Katie said in a husky voice.

"Anyway, Josh took off at a gallop. In the meantime, the boys got cold feet, and halfway there they turned around and came back. Of course, Josh had no way of knowing that." Morgan shook his head. "Somewhere near the site, the horse must have had an accident, because about an hour later the horse turned up at the barn, limping, and without Josh. I saddled up and went looking for him, but by then the construction workers had found him and had called an ambulance. They said they found him lying on the ground and that he was out cold."

The invisible hand squeezed Katie's heart tighter. "Didn't the paramedics tell you anything?"

"They were driving off by the time I got there," Morgan said. "I got back to the stables as fast as I could. The first person I saw was Chelsea. I told her and she told you. That's all I know. I'm sorry."

"Thank you for your quick action, Morgan," Mr. Holloway said.

Lacey shook her head. "Crazy kids. What were they thinking?"

"I'm sure they feel bad about it," Mr. Holloway said. "I'll talk to them when I return."

"Which looks like it may be never," Lacey grumbled. "I hate this place."

"It's a good hospital," Mr. Holloway said. "One of the best."

"It's where we brought Amanda. I'll never forget how terrible that experience was," Lacey added.

Neither would Katie. Nor would she forget how things had ended for Amanda. "Josh is a fighter," she said, mostly to encourage herself.

Mr. Holloway was told he had a phone call and went to answer it. When he returned, he told them,

"It was the camp. They're just checking to see if we know anything. Kimbra said Chelsea and Meg are watching your girls, so you stay as long as you like."

Katie wasn't about to leave, not until she saw Josh, not until she knew that he was going to be all right. She thought back to the other morning when they'd been together. Why hadn't she been nicer? Why hadn't she hugged him? What if she couldn't ever hug him again? She'd never forgive herself for the missed opportunity.

"What's taking so long?" Lacey asked.

Katie was grateful that Lacey was saying all the things she was thinking. Katie wanted to complain too but didn't have the energy. It was taking all her strength not to fall apart.

"Does anybody want anything?" Morgan asked. "I could go out for something."

Katie shook her head. She couldn't eat or drink a thing, afraid she'd throw up. All she wanted was to see Josh.

"This place gives me the creeps," Morgan said. He thought about the last time he'd seen his father in the institution where he was being maintained. Morgan's father hadn't known him, of course. Huntington's had reduced him to a helpless, slobbering, childlike being. Morgan had been horrified. And terrified too. What if that was going to happen to him?

He shook his head to clear it. He needed to concentrate on Josh, not on himself.

"How's the horse Josh was riding?" Katie asked.

"He was shaken up," Morgan explained, glad to be talking about something he understood and could control. "I got him into his stall and gave him a quick going over before I came here. His leg's swollen. He'll need to be looked at by a vet."

Mr. Holloway nodded. "Take care of it."

"Yes, sir."

Another hour passed. By now it was growing dark outside. Lights came on in the parking lot, and the patients in the emergency room came and went. The longer Katie waited with her friends, the more certain she became that something serious was wrong with Josh. They would have heard something by now if his injury had been simple.

Around eight o'clock a doctor stepped through the swinging doors of the triage area and asked, "Who's with Joshua Martel?"

Katie hurried to him, followed by the others. "How is he? What's wrong? Can I see him?" She was frantic with worry.

"I'm Dr. Harry Childs," the physician said. "I've

been treating Josh since he got here. Are you his family?"

"I'm responsible for him," Richard Holloway said. "He's working at the camp I'm running."

"I—We're his best friends," Katie said. "Tell us what's going on. Please."

"We've taken him upstairs," Dr. Childs said. "We've taken X rays and done an MRI. He'll need a CAT scan tomorrow."

"Is he . . . awake?"

"Yes, he's regained consciousness."

"That's good," Katie said hopefully.

The doctor looked serious. What was he not telling them?

"Josh has sustained a pretty severe injury to his neck and back."

"How serious?" Mr. Holloway asked.

"Evidently he went over the top of the horse he was riding. He landed here." The doctor grasped the lower back of his neck to illustrate his point. "Just below the top four vertebrae of his neck."

Katie's heart began to pound uncontrollably. "What does that mean?"

"Actually, it's too soon to tell, but you must be prepared."

"For what?"

"Josh may be permanently paralyzed."

SIXTEEN

Katie's knees buckled, and if Morgan and Lacey hadn't been standing on either side of her and hadn't caught her arms to steady her, she would have fallen. "You can't mean that!" she cried.

"It is a possibility," Dr. Childs said. "Until the swelling abates, we just won't know. Do you remember the actor Christopher Reeve, the one who played Superman?"

Katie remembered him well. She'd seen him on TV, speaking about spinal cord injuries from his wheelchair. That couldn't happen to Josh! "Yes," she said, her voice barely a whisper.

"Josh's injury is similar to Mr. Reeve's. Frankly, we just don't know yet how badly he's been hurt. It is a good sign that he's breathing on his own, that he doesn't need a ventilator. You see, the higher up the spinal cord the injury, the greater the extent of paralysis."

Katie shook her head. "No, that won't happen to Josh."

Dr. Childs looked sympathetic. "If his injury is incomplete, he can still recover. About half of all those injured do recover completely. Let's think positively, all right?"

"Does he know the extent of his injury yet?" Mr. Holloway asked.

"Not yet. He knows he's hurt pretty bad, but he doesn't know the rest of it. It can turn around for him, so there's no need to give him this kind of prognosis just now. A specialist will see him tomorrow. Dr. Benson is one of the best neurosurgeons in this area who treats this type of injury. Josh will be in excellent hands."

"I want him to have the best," Mr. Holloway said quietly.

Katie wiped her eyes. "I want to see him."

The doctor told her Josh's room number. "Keep in mind, he's been heavily sedated."

When the doctor walked away, Katie said to the others, "Not one bad word to Josh, understand? We can't let on that we know what we do."

"You go in first," Lacey said. "You're the only one he'll want to see, anyway."

Upstairs the corridor lights had been dimmed and the nurses' station was quiet. Katie found Josh's room, leaned against the door to gather herself, then went inside. Josh was lying flat on a hospital bed, strapped down and held rigid on a backboard. His head too was being held immobile. Katie crept to his side. He seemed to be asleep.

"Hi, Josh," she said softly.

His eyelids fluttered open. "Is that you, Katie?"

"It's me."

"Lean over the bed so I can see your face."

She complied. His pupils looked dilated, and his speech sounded somewhat slurred. "Are you in pain?" she asked.

"No pain. I feel like I'm floating."

"It's the medicine."

"You look pretty, Katie."

A lump the size of a fist clogged her throat. She cleared it away. "Lacey and Morgan and Mr. Holloway are waiting outside. They'd like to say hi to you."

"That's fine. Just as long as you're here, nothing else matters."

"I'll be here whenever you want me to be here, Josh. I won't let you go through this alone."

He managed a smile. "You'd better let the others come in, because I'm fading fast."

Katie called the others. Each of them leaned over the bed and wished Josh well.

"I'm sorry about the horse, Morgan," Josh said. "I hope he isn't hurt bad."

"He's fine."

"I don't know what happened. I was riding along and the next thing I knew, I was in the hospital. I'm embarrassed to think I got thrown."

"It happens." Morgan backed away.

"Mr. Holloway, how are my boys?"

"They're all right. Worried about you, but don't you worry about anything. Eric is moving into your cabin until you get back."

"Tell him not to get too settled in, 'cause I'll be back soon."

Katie almost broke out in a sob. Josh really didn't have any idea how grave his situation was. It broke her heart to hear him planning to get back to Jenny House Camp when she knew he might never return. At least, not on his own two legs.

"We'll let you get some rest now," Mr. Holloway said.

"I'll be back first thing in the morning," Katie promised.

"I'll be looking for you."

They left, and Katie made it to Lacey's car before

she broke down. She cried all the way back to camp, and in her cabin she cried late into the night. She promised herself that no matter what Josh's future was, she'd be there for him. Just as he had been there for her after her heart transplant.

Lacey let Katie drive her car to the hospital the next morning. She also divided up Katie's cabin of girls among herself, Meg, and Chelsea and promised to look after the girls for the remainder of the camp, if necessary. Katie was grateful to her friends for the way they were supporting her. All she could think about was Josh's grim possible prognosis. But when she walked into his room, she put on a happy face and acted as if everything were perfectly fine.

"Dr. Benson came in this morning," Josh told her. "He's started me on massive doses of steroids and anti-inflammatories." He motioned with his eyes toward the IV bag hanging on a pole beside his bed. "I'm going down for a CAT scan. It could take a while. Will you wait for me?"

"I'll be right here," she told him, and kissed his forehead.

"Thanks," he said quietly. "I needed that."

She squeezed his hand.

Once the orderly had wheeled him away, Katie

felt bereft. What if the worst had happened and Josh could never walk again? How would he take care of himself? What would he do? She thought about calling her parents and asking whether they would take Josh in until he could care for himself properly. They liked him a lot. Surely they would help him out.

"Katie?"

Katie turned and saw Sarah McGreggor standing in the doorway. "Well, hi," Katie said, surprised to see her. "How did you get here?"

"I begged Mr. Holloway to let me come with him. He's downstairs talking to the administrators. Lots of paperwork, I suppose."

"It's nice of you to come."

"I kept thinking about you. I knew your friends were helping out with your campers, so I decided to come and stay with you while Josh is going through all his testing."

Katie wondered how much Sarah knew about Josh's condition but decided that no one who knew the truth would have told her much. "How did you get away from Dullas?" Katie asked in an effort to lighten the mood.

"Lacey took Dullas on, and who's going to cross Lacey?"

"Good point."

Sarah sat in a chair and glanced around the room. "This is an odd position for me, you know. I'm usually the one in the bed everyone comes to visit."

"I remember when I was a patient," Katie said. "It felt weird to be stuck in bed. But my heart was so far gone, I didn't have much energy."

"I know what you mean. Before the bone marrow transplant, they had to wipe out my immune system. I was so exhausted, I couldn't move. Plus, I was in isolation and no one could come in or out without going through this whole sterilization procedure. My friends would send me presents and my mom would have to hold them up to the window that looked into my room and unwrap them for me because I couldn't come in contact with any germs."

"Yeah, it was the same way for me after my transplant—no germs."

Sarah chuckled. "What do you think regular girls talk about? I mean, listen to us. It's surgery, isolation, hospitals, bacteria-free environment . . . that doesn't sound like normal teenage conversation, does it?"

Katie smiled wearily. "You're right. It doesn't. I guess what we've lived through isn't very normal, though, is it?" She paused. "The truth is, everything that happened to me happened years ago. I hardly ever think about it anymore. All I know is that Josh has been with me every step of the way."

"You're lucky. I've spent so much time in and out of hospitals and going through one procedure or another . . . well, I can't forget it. For years it defined me. I hated it, but I couldn't get rid of it. Not even with the bone marrow transplant. I've wondered what it would be like to have a real life. To have a boyfriend."

Sarah sounded so wistful that it tugged at Katie's heart.

"I guess that's not the way things will go for me," Sarah added. "Guys aren't interested in girls with health problems."

"Guys eventually grow up and act mature," Katie said. "Someday you'll meet someone who will appreciate you just the way you are."

Sarah shook her head. "Maybe that happens in romance books. But not in real life. No, Katie, you're very lucky to have a guy like Josh. Hang on to him."

Long after Sarah was gone, Katie thought about her and the things she'd said. Poor Sarah! Would she ever feel normal? Katie hoped so.

When Josh returned to his room, he was so tired he didn't even want to eat his lunch, though Katie offered to feed it to him.

"I hate feeling so helpless," he said. "I can't even move my hands." He looked up at Katie with soulful, pleading eyes. "And, Katie, I didn't want to say anything this morning when you first came, but I can't feel my legs. They're numb. I can't feel them at all."

SEVENTEEN

"When Josh said that, I almost lost it in front of him." Katie was telling her closest friends about her visit to the hospital that morning. She'd returned to the camp only long enough to check on her responsibilities and to give Josh a chance to recuperate from his CAT scan. At camp things were running smoothly, although everyone asked her about Josh and when he might return.

"He still doesn't know anything about the seriousness of his fall?" Chelsea asked.

"He doesn't know the full potential of his injury yet," Katie said. "But he's catching on that it's nothing that's going to go away after a little bed rest."

"Have *you* talked to his neurosurgeon?" Lacey asked.

"No. I'd like to, but I don't know if he'd tell me anything or not."

"If he won't talk to you, I'm sure he's talking to Mr. Holloway," Meg said knowingly. "After all, he's the person in charge of Josh."

It irked Katie that she wasn't eligible to receive information firsthand about Josh, but she didn't let on. She did say, "I've gone to the hospital library and done some reading about spinal cord injury. Most times it's kids and teens who get injured—in car and motorcycle accidents, or in diving accidents, or playing sports. According to most articles, a lot of the accidents are because of just plain stupidity— driving drunk, or diving into shallow water. That's what makes it so hard to accept what happened to Josh. He wasn't doing anything wrong. He was trying to help somebody. It isn't fair he should be hurt this way."

"True," Lacey said. "Those two boys he set out to rescue are really upset. Both of them are nuts about Josh. They realize that if they hadn't been doing something wrong, he wouldn't have gotten hurt."

"They should have thought of that before they sneaked off," Katie said, feeling bitter.

"No one can foresee the future, Katie," Meg said. "The boys meant no harm. It was just a terrible accident."

Katie knew that what Meg said was true, but still she wanted to blame somebody. It had to be *some-*

body's fault. She grabbed up her purse and Lacey's car keys. "I'm going back to the hospital. The least I can do is keep Josh company. He's just miserable lying there all day long without being able to move."

Later that afternoon, she sat in Josh's room as he drifted in and out of drug-induced sleep. It was after dark and visiting hours were over when she kissed his forehead and promised to return the next morning.

"Thank you, Katie," Josh whispered. "Thank you for being here for me."

A fine red stubble grew on his face and felt rough against her hand when she stroked his cheek. "You were there for me," she reminded him. "I won't desert you, Josh."

Out in the hall, she ran into Mr. Holloway. He invited her down to the coffee shop and bought her a cup of coffee, getting coffee and a slice of pie for himself. When he'd settled into a chair across from her in the brightly lit room, he said, "I talked to Dr. Benson this afternoon."

The coffee turned bitter in Katie's mouth, and she set down the cup. "Are you going to give me bad news?"

"Actually, there's a little bit of encouraging

news," Mr. Holloway said. "Josh's score is rising on the motor function index."

"What's that?"

"It's a testing method for measuring how well a patient's motor skills are doing. A healthy person scores a hundred percent—there's no impairment of his motor skills. When Josh was brought in, his was at zero, which meant he couldn't even breathe on his own, but over the past two days his scores have risen."

"That's wonderful." She felt encouraged.

"Yes, but he's not out of the woods yet. According to Dr. Benson, the treatment they're giving Josh includes some experimental drugs, which, although they've proved effective in the lab, have a so-so track record with people. You see, the problem with the spinal cord is that after a severe trauma the nerve cells begin to die. Scientists have discovered that if they can stop this process, if they can keep the nerve cells alive, the victim has a better chance of avoiding paralysis. Or at least limiting it to perhaps only the lower part of his body."

Katie's eyes misted as the reality of Josh's situation sank in. "I just can't imagine Josh having to spend the rest of his life in a wheelchair."

"While it's true that half of these injuries lead to

paralysis, half of them don't. That's what you have to focus on. You're his encouragement, Katie. You help him keep a positive attitude, and no matter what the outcome, he's going to look to you to help him through this ordeal."

Katie dropped her gaze and stared into the cream-colored depths of her coffee cup. "We—We were closer once. I should have never cut myself off from him. Especially after all he did for me. If it weren't for his brother's heart, I wouldn't even be alive."

"You have a right to explore the possibilities for your own life. You have a right to discover who you are and what you want, Katie."

She looked up into Mr. Holloway's kind blue eyes. "I feel bad about the way I've treated him during the past year. I should have been nicer. Going away to college was so important to me this time last year. Right now it hardly seems important at all."

"You're a bright girl. Josh wouldn't want anybody who wasn't absolutely sure of what she wanted. When Jenny was alive, she was so much more positive about wanting me than I was about wanting her."

"Do you still miss her?"

"I'll always miss her. But I've had to go on with my life. I couldn't let all that she suffered count for nothing. Jenny House is her legacy. That's why I'm rebuilding, why I've fought so hard to keep her grandmother's dream alive. It's all I can do for them."

Katie understood what he was telling her. "When I was recovering from my transplant, when I wanted to run again but hardly had the strength to stand up, Josh took me on as his personal project. He never let me quit."

"That was then, this is now," Mr. Holloway said. "All that's behind you. You can't have a future if you can't let go of your past. Being there for Josh now shouldn't be out of gratitude for what he did for you. It should be out of what you feel for him in your heart."

Katie saw the subtle difference between the two things. Could she love Josh if he was trapped in a wheelchair? She didn't know the answer because she didn't know exactly what she felt for him. Pity? Yes. But pity couldn't carry her through the rest of her life. She couldn't be bound to someone because she felt sorry for him.

Mr. Holloway pushed away from the table. "It's late. We both should get back to camp."

"I have Lacey's car," Katie said. "I'll be coming soon. First I have a stop to make."

* * *

The full moon lit the construction site with a silvery glow. Katie parked and weaved her way through the well-trampled trail to the chapel. Much progress had been made since the first day of camp. She saw the shape of the building more clearly now. The building started low in the back, then rose higher in the front like the curving bow of a great boat. A partial roof was in place, but toward the front, where the altar and stained-glass window would be, the roof was still unfinished, and moonlight streamed through the opening. She stood in the moonlight, looking upward.

Tree frogs and katydids filled the air with their music; otherwise there was silence. Katie was alone. Utterly alone.

"Hello, God," she whispered. "It's me, Katie O'Roark." It had been so long since she'd prayed that she felt it necessary to reintroduce herself to the Creator.

"I—I need a favor." She stopped, collecting her thoughts. "It's not for me, you understand, but for Josh. You know he's hurt. He's hurt pretty bad. But I know you can fix him. With just a single word, you can make him well."

She remembered enough from her days in Sunday school to know that miracles happened. And that God was in charge of miracles. If he could raise

Lazarus from the dead and his son from a grave, then he could heal Josh's spinal cord.

She took a deep breath. She could make God a lot of promises, but she knew that would be futile. In the first place, even if she swore she'd be "good" for the rest of her life, she knew she couldn't keep such a vow. And God might not want her to swear such a thing. How could her being "good" possibly help Josh? No, she just needed to ask God outright to heal Josh.

An owl called from atop a nearby tree.

"Please make Josh all right," Katie pleaded, looking up at the sky. "Please, let him walk again. Not for me, but for himself. And if he has to be in a wheelchair, then help me to help him accept it. Give me the courage to stand by him the way he stood by me when I needed him."

She stopped. By now tears had filled her eyes and her heart felt as if it might break. She truly believed that God had heard her prayer. What she did not know was whether or not he would grant her request. Against great odds, God had given her a new heart when she'd desperately needed one. And he had brought Josh into her life as well. She believed that with all her heart and soul. Now there was nothing more she could do except wait. And have faith. Faith in God to hurry Josh's recovery. Faith in

Josh's ability to live bound to a wheelchair if he had
to. Either way, Josh's fate was in God's hands, in
God's mercy.

Katie lifted her arms in the moonlight in supplication to the heavens.

EIGHTEEN

"How's the horse doing?" Meg leaned over the half door of the stable to ask Morgan her question. She had walked down to the barn to visit him while the campers were having their weekly popcorn and movie night in the rec center.

Morgan, who was checking the horse's leg, stood up and came to the door. "He's still a little swollen around the knee, but the vet says he'll be okay."

"Good. I know how much these horses mean to you."

Morgan let himself out of the stall. "Any good word about Josh yet?" It had been three days since Josh's accident.

"Still waiting. Right after supper Katie headed straight back to the hospital. She says his doctor feels hopeful because Josh's X rays show no broken vertebrae or crushed discs. That means he won't have to undergo any surgery. He can still heal spontaneously."

Morgan picked up brushes from where he had been grooming the horses and motioned for Meg to follow him to the tack room. "Josh is tough, and . . . well, there are worse things than being paralyzed."

His comment surprised Meg, and she told him so. "I figured that as much as you like being outdoors and riding, you'd think being paralyzed would be one of the worst things in the world."

"I've seen wheelchair-bound athletes on TV. They move pretty good, and they look fit and tough to me. And just because you can't walk doesn't mean you can't ride."

His attitude continued to surprise her. She hadn't expected him to be so cavalier. "Well, I know I'd sure hate not being able to walk," she said.

His expression clouded and he got a faraway look in his eye. She couldn't imagine what was going through his mind. Was there someone in his life who was paralyzed? "Do you know anybody who—"

"Look, Meg, can we just drop it? I really don't want to talk about it."

She stepped back, shocked by his reaction. Why had he become defensive? He could be so moody. "I guess it was a mistake for me to come down here," she said quietly. "I'll see you tomorrow."

She'd taken only a few steps when he said, "Wait!" He caught up with her. "I'm sorry. I didn't mean to be rude. I'm glad you came to see me."

"You are?"

A smile tugged at the corners of his mouth. "I am." He took hold of her hand. "Let's walk."

They started down a trail in the woods. Daylight was fast fading, and lightning bugs were blinking among the leaves of the trees. "We never got to go on that moonlight ride, did we?" he asked.

"We were sidetracked."

"And now camp's closing in two weeks."

Meg felt let down. She could hardly imagine her days without the routine of camp life and seeing her new friends every day. And she couldn't imagine not seeing Morgan. "Will you go back to Colorado?" she asked.

"Sure. Winter's coming, and we'll have to bring the herds down from the high places and into the valley where there's better grazing. It's still a working ranch, and there's a lot to be done. What about you?"

"Back to Columbia. The books are calling to me. I haven't spent any time this summer studying."

"Why would you want to?"

She laughed. "Because I want to get into medical school. Only the brightest and best get in, you know."

"You'll make it," he said.

"Oh, really? And have you got a crystal ball that tells the future?"

He gave a short, derisive laugh. "If only."

She stopped and made him turn and face her. "What's going on with you, Morgan? Something is. You've said things to me that make me believe there's something you're not telling me about yourself."

Looking down at Meg's pretty upturned face made Morgan's insides turn mushy. What he wanted to do was take her in his arms and kiss her. But that wouldn't be fair. A girl like Meg deserved more than he could ever give her. She wanted to be a doctor. He didn't even know if he *had* a future.

"It's nothing," he said.

"I can take it." She persisted. "Do you have a fiancée tucked away somewhere you don't want me to know about?" She was teasing, but also serious. She wanted to get to the bottom of his secrecy.

"No fiancées," he said. "But . . ." He teetered on the brink of telling her. "It's personal."

"Do I have to play Twenty Questions? Let's

see . . ." She tapped her toe and thought up the most preposterous thing she could. "You've got some dread disease and you're dying."

She meant it as a joke, but when he didn't laugh, her heart began to thud with apprehension. "Morgan, I was just kidding."

"Actually, you're not too far off the mark," he said quietly.

"Please tell me."

He stepped away and, turning, quietly told her about his genetic potential for contracting Huntington's chorea. He hadn't told anyone since Anne, and he never talked about it with his aunt, the only relative he had left. His fears had been bottled up for so long that his voice shook as he spoke, but once he was through it, once he'd told Meg about its horrors, he felt a tremendous sense of release.

"And you've been living with this knowledge for almost eight years?" she asked, careful to keep her voice controlled and subdued. Inside she was reeling, but if there was one thing she had learned from her surgeon father, it was how to keep her voice calm and her expression serene. A patient must never see his doctor panic.

"Yes," Morgan answered.

"But you won't take the genetic test even though

you can afford it? Even though it would settle the matter once and for all?"

When she put it so matter-of-factly, his motives seemed petty. He confessed his darkest fear. "I—I'm afraid to."

He waited for her reaction, and when she neither scoffed nor scolded, he appreciated her even more.

"I would be afraid too," she said. "My mother has a friend who has a family history of breast cancer. The woman's scared to death she'll get it. There's a genetic test that can tell a woman if she carries the gene that might lead to her getting it. But even if she has the gene, there's no predicting absolutely that she'll get breast cancer. So she still has to 'wait and see.' Some women can't stand the suspense, so they have mastectomies anyway. My father won't do those surgeries. He thinks it's too drastic a measure."

Meg stared up at Morgan's clouded expression. "I think you're lucky to be able to take a simple test and know for sure whether or not you'll get Huntington's. Then all your waiting will be over."

"But what if it's positive? What if I am going to get it?"

"Then you can plan for it. Don't you think that's a whole lot better than wondering?"

"I'm not sure. Anne wanted me to take the test too."

"What if you don't get Huntington's, Morgan? How old will you be before you're absolutely, positively *sure* you won't get it?"

"It usually happens when you're in your thirties. Or maybe even when you're fifty."

"So then you'll live years never doing something you want to do, never getting married, or having children, just in case you *might* get sick? That's a long time to dangle your life, don't you think? And it doesn't seem fair to anybody who wants a future with you either."

"I try not to think about that," he said. "Keeping to myself, staying uninvolved, seems the best way for me to handle it."

Meg ran her palm down his arm and grasped his hand. "I would never tell you what to do, Morgan. It's your life, not mine. But I would think that living with *not* knowing is far more harmful than living with knowing. It eats you up inside. It does a kind of damage to your emotions and your spirit that dealing with the problem head-on avoids. Not facing the truth makes a person powerless. Knowledge is power, and the truth sets you free.

"If you're going to get Huntington's, you may as

well deal with it up front. Just like you do a wild horse. Would you not ride a horse because you might get thrown?"

"Of course not. I'd ride any wild horse."

"Then why not think of this genetic test as a wild horse? A big, scary one, but still just a wild horse that you can manage if you put your mind to it."

Meg's suggestion gave Morgan a new way of viewing his problem. He had avoided the truth for so long because he was afraid of it. And it was the only thing in his life he had ever been afraid of. "You'll make a hell of a doctor, Ms. Charnell," he said with a wry grin. "You've got a powerful way with words."

She shrugged. "It's up to you, but if you do take the test, will you please tell me the results?"

"If they're bad, I couldn't tell you. I don't want anybody's pity. Especially yours."

"And if they're good?"

He thought for a moment. "I could send you a yellow ribbon. *If* I take the test," he added.

She smiled up at him. "Fair enough," she said. Then she asked, "Will you write me?"

"I'll be out on the range most of the fall. Besides, I'm not much of a letter writer."

"I am. I'll write you whenever I feel like it. So there."

He laughed. "But there is something I will do."

"What's that?"

Morgan took her in his arms, tilted her chin up, and said with a kiss what he could not say with words.

NINETEEN

On the fourth day after Josh's accident, when Katie went to the hospital, she found him sitting in a wheelchair. He wore a stiff white neck brace, a cervical collar that held his neck straight and rigid.

"What do you think?" he asked when she stepped into the room.

"Wow, you're sitting up. That's progress." She was thrilled to see him out of bed, but the ominous sight of the chair made her stomach tighten.

"I have some feeling in my right arm, but my legs are pretty useless."

"Is that normal?" She wanted so much for him to get up and come to her.

"The doctor said so, but he's not telling me what I want to hear—that I can walk out of the hospital soon." Josh grimaced. "I sure hate this collar. I have to turn my whole body if I want to look to the right or left. But it helps keep my neck straight, and Dr. Benson doesn't want it to get jarred."

"How long will you have to wear it?"

"It depends. Six weeks to three months."

"What happens next?"

"They haven't said. I'm going down to rehab, though, and that seems like a good sign to me."

She came closer. "You work really hard in rehab, you hear?"

"Katie, I know how serious my injury was."

"You do?" Her gaze flew to his face. Her instinct was to protect him.

"I know they aren't sure if I'll walk again."

Tears misted her eyes, and she turned away.

"Hey," he said softly, "it's not going to happen to me. I won't let it."

"You were really hurt bad, Josh."

"I know. Dr. Benson's been honest with me, and I'm glad. I know you've been scared for me, haven't you?"

She nodded, not trusting her voice.

"You don't have to keep it inside now," Josh told her. "I know the worst. But I'm not afraid. The treatments they gave me helped a lot. Now I believe the rest is up to me. There are football players who've had injuries like mine—worse than mine—

and they were told they'd never walk again, and now, a few years later, they're up walking and going to the gym.

"I'm not saying it's going to be easy, but I can do this, Katie. Dr. Benson told me that the higher up the spinal cord the damage occurs, the greater the chance of complete paralysis. And that while I went over the horse and bent my neck pretty bad, it was the middle of my back that took the brunt of the fall."

"And that's a good thing?"

"It left me with upper-body movement. Watch."

She looked down at his hands and saw the barest twitch of his thumbs. For the first time that morning, she smiled. "Why, that's wonderful!"

"My legs are the most affected," Josh continued. "They're not sure if I'll get full use of them back, but I'm here to tell you—I will."

She saw determination on his face and believed him.

"When I get home, I have to go into physical therapy. I may not get back to classes till after Christmas."

"How will you manage on your own?"

"Like I always have," he said. "I'll manage."

"I wish I didn't have to go back to school. I could help."

"Is this Katie talking? Katie, who couldn't wait to get back to Arizona and run track?"

Her cheeks burned at his gentle chiding. Funny how her priorities had shifted over the past several days. Now, instead of school, all she could think about was how Josh was going to make it by himself. "I don't want you to be alone."

"Katie, look at me."

She did, and his blue eyes burned brightly. He said, "I have never wanted to stand in the way of your dreams. I won't let this accident sidetrack you in any way. Go back to school. Have a good time. I'll be all right."

"I suppose Natalie could help you," she ventured, feeling the the familiar prickling of jealousy in her heart.

"She's a good friend. But she's only a friend. And yes, she'll help me."

Katie wasn't mollified. What if Josh's friendship with Natalie turned into something more?

The door opened, and a man dressed in white stepped into the room. "I'm John, your therapist," he said. "Ready to go down to rehab?"

"Ready and wanting to get started," Josh said.

"That's the attitude," John said with a smile.

"I'll wait for you," Katie said.

"It's all right," Josh answered. "I've got to learn

to do this on my own. Go on back to camp and tell everyone I'm doing better."

Katie watched the therapist push Josh in his wheelchair out of the room. She felt bereft and lost.

Only two days before the end of camp, Josh was released from the hospital. The entire camp threw a big party in the rec center. Banners proclaiming WELCOME BACK, JOSH! were strung across the room, and helium balloons hugged the ceiling. Eric had baked a giant sheet cake, and the staff had tacked to one wall an enormous piece of butcher paper, which every kid at camp had drawn pictures and written messages on.

When Josh arrived in the late afternoon, still in a wheelchair, everyone clustered around him. "It's good to be back," he told them all.

One of the boys asked what was on all their minds. "Will you be all right?"

"They think so," Josh answered.

"Can you walk?" asked another.

"I can stand with help, but it hurts."

"Your arm doesn't move so well," a girl noted.

"I'm still working out the kinks," he told her.

"Can you stay with us, or do you have to go back to the hospital?" another boy asked.

"I'm here to stay."

A cheer went up. Music began to play, and games started. Katie stuck close to Josh, but she wasn't at all sure he wanted her with him. A subtle shift had occurred. She couldn't say exactly what was different, but things between them were different. It was as if Josh had released her in some way. As if he'd let go of their relationship. He was kind to her, but she no longer felt tied to him emotionally. Neither did she experience the old gnawing guilt when she was around him, as if she owed him something, a debt she couldn't pay. The feelings disturbed her, but she couldn't say why.

Later she stepped outside and breathed in the humid Carolina night air. Dampness mingled with the scent of jasmine, making her feel melancholy. Summer was nearly over. Soon she'd return to college and resume her other life. Yet this life had come to mean so much to her.

"Hey, Katie."

She turned and saw Sarah. "Hey yourself."

"You want to be alone?"

She did, but she would never tell that to Sarah. "Not at all. I was just taking a break."

Sarah leaned against the wall next to her. "I can't believe it's almost time to go home. When camp first started, I couldn't wait for it to end. Now I don't want it to."

"I know. It's that way every year for me, Lacey, and Chelsea. After the campers leave, we pull an all-nighter where we eat and talk and cry because it's all over and we have to go back home."

"Sounds like fun." Sarah's voice was wistful.

Katie studied Sarah's face, and an idea came to her. "If you were a counselor you could stay with us."

"I'm not a counselor."

"Would you like to be?"

Sarah's eyes widened. "What do you mean?"

"Every year we make recommendations to Mr. Holloway as to who we think would make good counselors. I'd like to recommend you. You'd make a fabulous counselor next year."

"You mean it?"

"I wouldn't have said anything if I didn't."

"Really?" Sarah's face broke into a grin. In the moonlight she looked pretty but fragile. "I'd love to be a counselor here!" she cried.

"Next year it'll be a whole lot better because the main camp will be rebuilt. The dorms over there are posh, not like the cabins at all. You'll have a great time, Sarah."

"What about you? Won't you be back? I can't imagine this place without you, Katie."

Katie glanced through the window and saw Josh

talking to a group of kids. Sadness tugged at her heart. Everything was changing. She knew that as surely as she knew her own name. "Probably not, Sarah," she said quietly. "I think it's time I moved on. I think it's time for me to leave Jenny House for others, for girls like you. It's . . . time to say good-bye."

TWENTY

Chaos ruled the campground as parents arrived to pick up their kids on the last day of Jenny House camp. Some kids were crying because they didn't want to leave. Katie tried to comfort them while at the same time trying to make sure everybody had all their belongings.

Once the campers were gone, the staff would have a meeting; then Katie and her friends would spend one final night together, with popcorn, fudge, cookies, sodas, and ice cream to console them. "I'll gain back every ounce I've lost," Meg wailed.

"Yeah, but what a way to go," Chelsea told her.

Lacey insisted on boosting her insulin dosage so that she could join them in the pigout.

Because Sarah wanted to become a counselor, she called her parents and asked if they could come for her the next day. They agreed, saying they would spend the night at a motel in town and pick her up the following morning. Now she could spend the last night with Katie, Meg, Lacey, and Chelsea.

Katie was saying goodbye to the last of her girls when Dullas found her. "Me and Kimbra are leaving."

"We'll miss you," Katie said.

"Do you mean that?"

Katie thought for a moment. "I do. You were actually pretty tame this year. You must be growing up, Dullas."

Dullas made a face. Katie noticed that she wasn't wearing her pendant and asked about it. She'd never seen Dullas without it. "You haven't lost it, have you? You know how special it is to all of us."

"I didn't lose it. I—um—gave it to Sarah. I told her she could wear it all year and bring it back to me next year. She's my best friend, you know."

"Did you tell her the history behind it?"

"Course. She knows it's special. She'll take good care of it."

Katie was sure of that. Sarah was the perfect person to take Amanda's diamond for safekeeping. "Well, I think that's very unselfish of you, Dullas."

Dullas beamed with pleasure.

Because Josh couldn't drive his truck home, he was to fly out the next morning. Eric had volunteered to drive the truck up to Michigan for him and stay on for a few days' visit.

Katie was flying home herself, but she hadn't been able to get on the same plane as Josh, so she would leave later in the afternoon. Her parents would be at the airport to meet Josh and make sure he got home safely.

By suppertime the camp was quiet, all but deserted. The few remaining staff and counselors ate a lonely meal in the rec center. Meg excused herself, promising to return in time for their party.

"Morgan's leaving in the morning," she said. "I want to tell him goodbye."

"Oh, all right," Lacey said. "So Katie, Sarah, Chelsea, and I will start without you. Don't blame us if your fudge portion is skimpy."

"Listen, I'll be late too," Chelsea said. "Eric's asked me to go on a moonlight canoe ride with him and I'm going." She looked effervescent.

"Well, that's just peachy." Lacey crossed her arms and pouted. "Come on, Katie and Sarah, we'll eat *all* the fudge."

"Actually," Katie said, "I was going to ask if I could borrow your car for a little while. I want to take Josh someplace special before we leave."

*　*　*

"This is where I came when you were in the hospital."

Katie had coaxed Josh's wheelchair across the bumpy path to the Jenny House Chapel, and now they were alone in the moonlight, looking up at the splendid structure from the inside.

"Impressive," Josh said.

She moved the chair back so that he could get a better view of the soaring front of the structure.

"Why did you come?" he asked.

"I wanted to ask God to make you well. This seemed the best place to do it."

He caught her hand. "Thank you, Katie. That was a nice thing to do."

"I didn't do it to be nice. I did it because I care about you."

"I used to ask God to make you well too. That time when you got so sick and we thought you were rejecting your heart transplant . . . well, I really prayed hard then."

The moonlight glinted silver off the frame of the wheelchair. "I've tried so hard to take care of Aaron's heart for you," she added. She felt like crying.

"Katie, please listen to me. It's not Aaron's heart. It's *your* heart. And it has been since the moment your blood began to pour through it. I gave my brother's heart away without ever knowing who would get it. The fact that it was you makes no difference. There are no strings attached to the gift. There never were. There never will be."

What they were talking about had happened years before. Katie didn't know why she wanted to speak of it now. She thought they'd finished with it, but apparently not. "When you were in the hospital," she said, "when I realized how hurt you were, I discovered something."

"Which was . . . ?"

She took a deep breath. "I discovered that I love you . . . really love you. And that I don't want to go through the rest of my life without you."

Josh didn't say anything for a long time. Katie's heart hammered. Was she too late? Had his feelings for her changed so much that he no longer loved her?

"I let you go last summer, Katie. I made up my mind that I wasn't going to hold you back. Now I've had an accident and you feel sorry for me—"

"No," she interrupted. "If you never walk again, it won't change how I feel about you."

"You picked a fine time to tell me," he said with a short laugh. "When I can't stand up or turn my head. Or kiss you the way I'd like to."

She crouched in front of him. "Then allow me," she said. She slid her arms around him and bent forward until their lips touched in the moonlight.

"Well, it's about time," Lacey declared the minute Katie strolled into the cabin. "I thought we were going to have to send out a search party."

"I'm here now. What's left to eat?"

"We were just about to head over to the rec center and raid the ice cream freezer," Chelsea said, popping a chunk of chocolate chip cookie into her mouth. "And now I have to tell the story of my canoe ride all over again because you missed it the first time."

Katie eased onto a bed. The others sat on the floor in a circle. "I'm all ears."

"What's with you, anyway?" Lacey studied Katie intently.

"What?"

Lacey's eyes narrowed. "You look like you're going to pop if you don't tell us something."

"You're exaggerating."

"You look that way to me too," Meg said.

"Me too," Sarah added.

"All right, Katie O'Roark," Lacey said, crossing her arms over her chest. "Tell us what's going on. Spill it."

Katie faked a yawn. "Oh, all right, but you've got to promise me that you won't yell and scream and jump up and down like wild women."

The girls exchanged glances and shrugs.

"Okay, we promise," Lacey said, acting as spokesperson.

Katie leaned forward. "Next June, in Jenny Chapel, Josh and I are getting married. And I want all of you to be my bridesmaids."

The girls broke their promise.

TWENTY-ONE

"Are you going to write about today in your sports column?" Katie asked as she studied her reflection in the full-length mirror. Her father stood behind her dressed in a black tuxedo, a white carnation in his lapel.

"You bet I will. I've written about you in that column since the day you were born. Why stop now?"

"And just what has my wedding day got to do with sports?" she teased.

He thought a moment, then said, "I'm being a good sport. I'm letting that young man take you away from me."

"Oh, Daddy . . . ," she said with a smile.

He glanced at his watch for the hundredth time. "I'd better go up and check on the groomsmen."

"Afraid Josh won't show up?"

"No . . . afraid he will."

Katie laughed and shoved him toward the stairs, then turned back to the mirror. Her stomach felt as if a thousand butterflies had set up camp inside, but in the mirror, in the magnificent white satin gown studded with seed pearls and sequins, she looked calmly elegant. *Is this really me?* she wondered, staring at her reflection. Was she really going to become Mrs. Joshua Martel in less than an hour?

The previous September she had returned to Arizona, but at midterm she'd transferred to the University of Michigan, where the track coach had offered her a generous scholarship for the following year.

Since January she had lived with her parents, attended classes, spent every minute she could with Josh, and planned her wedding. Josh had completed a rigorous rehab program, and now, almost a year after his accident, had made a remarkable recovery. He had only a slight limp. After their honeymoon in Aruba, they would live in his grandfather's house. Katie and her mother had already fixed it up with new curtains, new kitchen and bathroom wallpaper and paint, and some new furniture.

Katie, Josh, and her family had spent the previous week in North Carolina tending to last-minute details for the wedding. Katie's bridesmaids had arrived two days before. Josh's parents had come too. Katie had never met them before, and even though Josh had been anxious about having them around, they seemed to be on their best behavior. So far they had stayed sober, and the previous night had sponsored a wonderful rehearsal dinner for the wedding party.

Josh had asked Richard Holloway to be his best man. Katie thought it fitting. And Mr. Holloway had pulled them aside at the rehearsal dinner and said, "Thank you. This is an honor for me. I find it very gratifying that the first event to be held in Jenny Chapel is a wedding. My Jenny would have loved knowing that."

Katie's heart had gone out to him, for surely he must have wondered what his life would have been like if Jenny had lived and they had married.

Katie turned to the sound of her bridesmaids giggling together in the corner. Lacey was fixing Chelsea's hair while Meg and Tara, Katie's college roommate from Arizona, stood offering advice. Katie thought they looked beautiful in their pale lilac gowns, and she only wished Sarah could have been with them.

Sarah had died in the spring. Her bone marrow transplant had failed, and there had been nothing else the doctors could do for her. Katie would never forget the night Sarah's mother called to tell her the news.

"I can't believe it," Katie had sobbed into the receiver. "I wanted her in my wedding so much."

"She tried very hard to make it. But her body just broke down. We buried her in the bridesmaid dress," Sarah's mother said in her soft Southern drawl. "She looked lovely. Everyone said so."

"I'll miss her," Katie said, still crying. "We all will."

"She was so looking forward to your wedding, Katie. It kept her going, made her last days more bearable. We will always be grateful she had you in her life, and the friends she made at camp last summer."

Sarah's mother paused. "Listen, dear, I'm mailing you something that Sarah wanted you to have. She said you'd understand."

Now, remembering that April evening, Katie reached up and fingered the diamond pendant around her neck. It had come full circle, back to Jenny House. She believed that Amanda would be pleased to know Katie was wearing it as her "something borrowed" on her wedding day. Katie wore the necklace for Sarah, for Amanda, for Jillian, and for all of them.

"Are we ready?" The wedding director, a small

woman with brown hair, came hurrying into the room.

The bridesmaids and the bride scurried over to her. "Here we go," Lacey said.

"Hope I don't trip," Chelsea said.

"I hope I don't faint," Meg countered.

"Go, girl," Tara said to Katie.

Katie hugged each of her bridesmaids. "I'll be right behind you," she promised, and watched them line up as they were to walk down the aisle in front of her: Tara, Chelsea, and Meg, followed by Lacey, the maid of honor.

"You all look lovely," the director said with a bright smile. She turned to Katie. "Your father's waiting at the top of the stairs."

Katie watched her friends climb the carpeted stairway to the vestibule. As Meg walked up, Katie again caught sight of her odd choice of necklace. Meg wore a yellow grosgrain ribbon tied at the back of her neck. A locket hung from the ribbon against her throat. "My grandmother's," she'd explained earlier.

"Wouldn't it look better on a gold chain?" Lacey had asked. "I can loan you one if you'd like."

Meg had reached up and touched the ribbon. "If you don't mind, I'd rather wear this. It was a gift from a friend. A special gift."

Katie had said, "Wear it."

Katie took a deep breath and climbed the stairs behind her friends, the wedding director carrying her long train. In the narthex, her father stepped up and patted her hand. The director smoothed Katie's train and fluffed her veil. The music started, and Lacey began her walk down the carpeted aisle. One by one the other girls followed.

From her vantage point, Katie saw the chapel pews filled with her family and friends. At the front of the chapel, behind the granite altar, the stained-glass window soared in hues of blue, yellow, and green. The center pane depicted white orchids, Jenny Crawford's favorite flower, and above that pane was a blazing emblem of the sun. At the bottom, in Gothic-style lettering, was a passage from Scripture: "Lo, I am with you always."

Light flooded through the window and cast the chapel in shades of pale blue and yellow. The scent of summer flowers hung in the cool mountain air.

The minister stood on the altar steps, and beside him Katie saw her Josh, smiling. Next to Josh stood his groomsmen—Richard Holloway, Jeff, Eric, and Morgan. A lump filled her throat and tears misted her eyes as she watched the procession. Her heart swelled. She loved them so! There could be no better friends in all the world. She wished Jenny Crawford could see from heaven all the good she had given to the world. The thought that maybe she could made Katie beam.

The organist began the wedding processional from *Lohengrin,* and Katie's father asked, "Ready, lovely Katie?"

"Very ready, Daddy."

She took her father's arm, and with her gaze locked on to Josh's, Katie O'Roark walked toward her future.

Dear Reader,

or those of you who have been longtime readers, I
hope you have enjoyed this newest One Last Wish
volume. For those of you discovering One Last Wish for the
first time, I hope you will want to read the other books that
are listed in detail in the next few pages. You'll be able to
read the stories of the characters who have come together in
this volume. From Lacey to Katie to Morgan and the rest,
you'll discover the lives of the characters I hope you've come
to care about just as I have.

Since the series began, I have received numerous letters
from teens wishing to volunteer at Jenny House. That is not
possible because Jenny House exists only in my imagination,
but there are many fine organizations and camps for sick
kids that would welcome volunteers. If you are interested in
becoming such a volunteer, contact your local hospitals
about their volunteer programs or try calling service organizations in your area to find out how you can help. Your own
school might have a list of community service programs.

Extending yourself is one of the best ways of expanding
your world . . . and of enlarging your heart. Turning good
intentions into actions is consistently one of the most re-
warding experiences in life. My wish is that the ideals of
Jenny House will be carried on by you, my reader. I hope
that now that we share the Jenny House attitude, you will
believe as I do that the end is often only the beginning.

Thank you for caring.

YOU'LL WANT TO READ ALL THE ONE LAST WISH
BOOKS BY BESTSELLING AUTHOR

Let Him Live
Someone Dies, Someone Lives
Mother, Help Me Live
A Time to Die
Sixteen and Dying
Mourning Song
The Legacy: Making Wishes Come True
Please Don't Die
She Died Too Young
All the Days of Her Life
A Season for Goodbye
Reach for Tomorrow

$\mathcal{I}$F YOU WANT TO KNOW MORE ABOUT MEGAN,

BE SURE TO READ

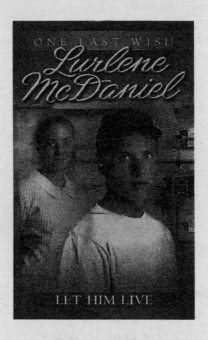

ON SALE NOW FROM BANTAM BOOKS
0-553-56067-0

Excerpt from *Let Him Live* by Lurlene McDaniel
Copyright © 1993 by Lurlene McDaniel

Published by Bantam Doubleday Dell Books for Young Readers
a division of Random House, Inc.
1540 Broadway, New York, New York 10036

*B*eing a candy striper isn't Megan Charnell's idea of an exciting summer, but she volunteered and can't get out of it. Megan has her own problems to deal with. Still, when she meets Donovan Jacoby, she find herself getting involved in his life.

Donovan shares with Megan his secret: An anonymous benefactor has granted him one last wish, and he needs Megan's help. The money can't buy a compatible transplant, but it can allow Donovan to give his mother and little brother something he feels he owes them. Can Megan help make his dream come true?

"When I first got sick in high school, kids were pretty sympathetic, but the sicker I got and the more school I missed, the harder it was to keep up with the old crowd," Donovan explained. "Some of them tried to understand what I was going through, but unless you've been really sick . . ." He didn't finish the sentence.

"I've never been sick," Meg said, "but I really do know what you're talking about."

He tipped his head and looked into her eyes. "I believe you do."

*I*F YOU WANT TO KNOW MORE ABOUT

KATIE AND JOSH, BE SURE TO READ

ON SALE NOW FROM BANTAM BOOKS
0-553-29842-9

Excerpt from *Someone Dies, Someone Lives* by Lurlene McDaniel
Copyright © 1992 by Lurlene McDaniel

Published by Bantam Doubleday Dell Books for Young Readers
a division of Random House, Inc.
1540 Broadway, New York, New York 10036

$\mathcal{K}$atie O'Roark feels miserable, though she knows she's incredibly lucky to have received an anonymous gift of money. The money can't buy the new heart she needs or bring back her days as a track star.

A donor is found with a compatible heart, and Katie undergoes transplant surgery. While recuperating, she meets Josh Martel and senses an immediate connection. When Katie decides to start training to realize her dream of running again, Josh helps her meet the difficult challenge.

Will Katie find the strength physically and emotionally to live and become a winner again?

From the corner of her eye, Katie saw a boy with red hair who was about her age. He stood near the doorway, looking nervous. With a start, she realized he was watching her because he kept averting his gaze when she glanced his way. Odd, Katie told herself. Katie had a nagging sense she couldn't place him. As nonchalantly as possible, she rolled her wheelchair closer, picking up a magazine as she passed a table.

She flipped through the magazine, pretending to be interested, all the while glancing discreetly toward the boy. Even though he also picked up a magazine, Katie could tell that he was preoccupied with studying her. Suddenly, she grew self-conscious. Was something wrong with the way she looked? She'd thought she looked better than she had in months when she'd left her hospital room that afternoon. Why was he watching her?

Katie is also featured in the novels *Please Don't Die, She Died Too Young,* and *A Season for Goodbye.*

*I*F YOU WANT TO KNOW MORE ABOUT SARAH,

BE SURE TO READ

ON SALE NOW FROM BANTAM BOOKS
0-553-29811-9

Excerpt from *Mother, Help Me Live* by Lurlene McDaniel
Copyright © 1992 by Lurlene McDaniel

Published by Bantam Doubleday Dell Books for Young Readers
a division of Random House, Inc.
1540 Broadway, New York, New York 10036

*S*arah McGreggor is distraught when she learns she will need a bone marrow transplant to live. And she is shocked to find out that her parents and siblings can't be donors because they aren't her blood relatives. Sarah never knew she was adopted.

As Sarah faces this devastating news, she is granted one last wish by an anonymous benefactor. With hope in her heart, she begins a search for her birth mother, who gave her up fifteen years ago. Sarah's life depends on her finding this woman. But what will Sarah discover about the true meaning of family?

Didn't the letter from JWC say she could spend it on anything she wanted? What could be more important than finding her birth mother? What could be more important than discovering if she had siblings with compatible bone marrow? Her very life could depend on finding these people. Sarah practically jumped up from the sofa. "I've got to go," she said.

𝒥F YOU WANT TO KNOW MORE ABOUT ERIC,

BE SURE TO READ

ON SALE NOW FROM BANTAM BOOKS
0-553-29809-7

Excerpt from *A Time to Die* by Lurlene McDaniel
Copyright © 1992 by Lurlene McDaniel

Published by Bantam Doubleday Dell Books for Young Readers
a division of Random House, Inc.
1540 Broadway, New York, New York 10036

*S*ixteen-year-old Kara Fischer has never considered herself lucky. She doesn't understand why she was born with cystic fibrosis. Despite her daily treatments, each day poses the threat of a lung infection that could put her in the hospital for weeks. But her close friendship with her fellow CF patient Vince and the new feelings she is quickly developing for Eric give her the hope to live one day at a time.

When an anonymous benefactor promises to grant a single wish with no strings attached, Kara finds a way to let the people who have loved and supported her throughout her illness know how much they mean to her. But will there be time for Kara to see her dying wish fulfilled?

"What am I going to do about you, Kara?"

Eric's tone was subdued and so sincere that his question caught her by surprise. "What do you mean?"

"I can't stay away from you."

"You seem to be doing a fine job of it," she said quietly, but without malice.

"I know it seems that way, but you don't know how hard it's been."

She was skeptical. "We just danced together, but after tonight, how will it be between us? Will you still ignore me in the halls? Will you duck into the nearest open door whenever you see me coming?"

He turned his head and she saw his jaw clench. She thought he might walk away, but instead he asked, "What's between you and Vince?"

IF YOU WANT TO KNOW MORE ABOUT MORGAN,

BE SURE TO READ

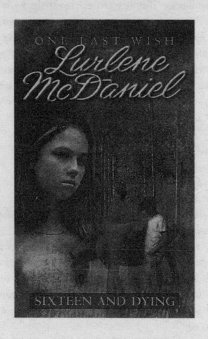

ON SALE NOW FROM BANTAM BOOKS
0-553-29932-8

Excerpt from *Sixteen and Dying* by Lurlene McDaniel
Copyright © 1992 by Lurlene McDaniel

Published by Bantam Doubleday Dell Books for Young Readers
a division of Random House, Inc.
1540 Broadway, New York, New York 10036

𝒯t's hard for Anne Wingate and her father to accept the doctors' diagnosis: Anne is HIV-positive. Seven years ago, before blood screening was required, Anne received a transfusion. It saved her life then, but now the harsh reality can't be changed—the blood was tainted. Anne must deal with the inevitable progression of her condition.

When an anonymous benefactor promises to grant Anne a single wish with no strings attached, she decides to spend the summer on a ranch out west. She wants to live as normally as she possibly can. The summer seems even better than she dreamed, especially after she meets Morgan. Anne doesn't confide in Morgan about her condition and doesn't plan to. Then her health begins to deteriorate and she returns home. Is there time for Anne and Morgan to meet again?

Fearfully, Anne stared at her bleeding hand.

Morgan reached beneath her, lifted her, and placed her safely away from the hay and its invisible weapon. "Let me see how bad you're cut."

"It's nothing," Anne said, keeping her hand close to her body. "I'm fine."

"You're not fine. You're bleeding. You may need stitches. Let me wipe it off and examine it."

Her eyes widened, reminding him of a deer trapped in headlights. "No! Don't touch it!"

"But—"

"Please—you don't understand. I—I can't explain. Just don't touch it." Wild-eyed, panicked, she spun, and clutching her hand to her side, she bolted from the barn.

Dumbfounded, Morgan watched her run back toward the cabin.

You MAY ALSO WANT TO READ

On Sale Now from Bantam Books
0-553-29810-0

Excerpt from *Mourning Song* by Lurlene McDaniel
Copyright © 1992 by Lurlene McDaniel

Published by Bantam Doubleday Dell Books for Young Readers
a division of Random House, Inc.
1540 Broadway, New York, New York 10036

𝒯t's been months since Dani Vanoy's older sister, Cassie, was diagnosed as having a brain tumor. And now the treatments aren't helping. Dani is furious that she is powerless to help her sister. She can't even convince their mother to take the girls on the trip to Florida Cassie has always longed for.

Then Cassie receives an anonymous letter offering her a single wish. Dani knows she can never make Cassie well, but she is determined to see Cassie's dream come true, with or without their mother's approval.

Dani had rehearsed the speech so many times that even she was beginning to believe it. "It's as if you're supposed to do this. While we don't know who gave you the money for a wish, I think you should use it to get something you've always wanted. Listen, even a trillion dollars can't make you well, but the money you've gotten can help you have some fun. I say let's go for it! You deserve to see the ocean, whether Mom agrees or not. I'm going to help you make your wish come true."

$\mathcal{I}$F YOU WANT TO KNOW MORE ABOUT RICHARD
HOLLOWAY AND JENNY CRAWFORD,

BE SURE TO READ

ON SALE NOW FROM BANTAM BOOKS
0-553-56134-0

Excerpt from *The Legacy: Making Wishes Come True* by Lurlene McDaniel
Copyright © 1993 by Lurlene McDaniel

Published by Bantam Doubleday Dell Books for Young Readers
a division of Random House, Inc.
1540 Broadway, New York, New York 10036

*W*ho is JWC, and how was the One Last Wish Foundation created? Follow JWC's struggle for survival against impossible odds and the intertwining stories of love and friendship that developed into a legacy of giving. And discover the power that one individual's determination can have, in this extraordinary novel of hope.

"I had my physician call the ER doctor and afterward, when we discussed their conversation, he suggested that I get her to a specialist as quickly as possible."

"A specialist at Boston Children's," Richard said with a nod. "What kind of specialist?"

"A pediatric oncologist."

Before Richard could say another word, Jenny's grandmother spoke. "A cancer specialist," Marian said, her voice catching. "They believe Jenny has leukemia."

*I*F YOU WANT TO KNOW MORE ABOUT KATIE,
CHELSEA, AND LACEY,
BE SURE TO READ

ON SALE NOW FROM BANTAM BOOKS
0-553-56262-2

Excerpt from *Please Don't Die* by Lurlene McDaniel
Copyright © 1993 by Lurlene McDaniel

Published by Bantam Doubleday Dell Books for Young Readers
a division of Random House, Inc.
1540 Broadway, New York, New York 10036

*W*hen Katie O'Roark receives an invitation from the One Last Wish Foundation to spend the summer at Jenny House, she eagerly says yes. Katie is ever grateful to JWC, the unknown person who gave her the gift that allowed her to receive a heart transplant. Now Katie is asked to be a "big sister" to others who, like her, face daunting medical problems: Amanda, a thirteen-year-old victim of leukemia; Chelsea, a fourteen-year-old candidate for a heart transplant; and Lacey, a sixteen-year-old diabetic who refuses to deal with her condition. As the summer progresses, the girls form close bonds and enjoy the chance to act "just like healthy kids." But when a crisis jeopardizes one girl's chance of fulfilling her dreams, they discover true friendship and its power to endure beyond this life.

"Me, too. I don't know what I'd do without you, Katie. Whenever I think about last summer, about how you were so close to dying . . ."

She didn't allow him to complete his sentence. "Every day is new, every morning, Josh. I'm glad I got a second chance at life. And after meeting the people here at Jenny House, after making friends with Amanda, Chelsea, and even Lacey, I want all of us to live forever."

He grinned. "Forever's a long time."

She returned his smile. "All right, then at least until we're all old and wrinkled."

𝒥F YOU WANT TO KNOW MORE ABOUT
KATIE AND CHELSEA, BE SURE TO READ

ON SALE NOW FROM BANTAM BOOKS
0-553-56263-0

Excerpt from *She Died Too Young* by Lurlene McDaniel
Copyright © 1994 by Lurlene McDaniel

Published by Bantam Doubleday Dell Books for Young Readers
a division of Random House, Inc.
1540 Broadway, New York, New York 10036

Chelsea James and Katie O'Roark met at Jenny House and spent a wonderful summer together.

Now Chelsea and her mother are staying with Katie as Chelsea awaits news about a heart transplant. While waiting for a compatible donor, Chelsea meets Jillian, a kind, funny girl who's waiting for a heart-lung transplant. The two girls become fast friends. When Chelsea meets Jillian's brother, he awakens feelings in her she's never known before. But as her medical situation grows desperate, Chelsea finds herself in a contest for her life against her best friend. Is it fair that there's a chance for only one of them to survive?

"Don't you see? There's one donor coming in. Only one. Who will the doctors save? Who will get the transplant?"

For a moment Josh stared blankly as her question sank in. "Katie, you don't know for sure there's only one donor."

"Yes, I do. There's only one. One heart. Two lungs. The doctor said the donor's family had given permission for all her organs to be donated." Katie's voice had risen with the tide of panic rising in her. "There's two people in need and only one heart."

Katie and Chelsea are also featured in the novels *Please Don't Die* and *A Season for Goodbye*.

$\mathcal{I}$F YOU WANT TO KNOW MORE ABOUT LACEY,

BE SURE TO READ

ON SALE NOW FROM BANTAM BOOKS
0-553-56264-9

Excerpt from *All the Days of Her Life* by Lurlene McDaniel
Copyright © 1994 by Lurlene McDaniel

Published by Bantam Doubleday Dell Books for Young Readers
a division of Random House, Inc.
1540 Broadway, New York, New York 10036

Out of control—that's how Lacey Duval feels in almost every aspect of her life. There's nothing she can do about her parents' divorce, there's nothing she can do about the death of her young friend, there's nothing she can do about having diabetes—that's what Lacey believes.

After a special summer at Jenny House, Lacey is determined to put her problems behind her. When she returns to high school, she is driven to become a part of the in crowd. But Lacey thinks fitting in means losing weight and hiding her diabetes. She starts skipping meals and experimenting with her medication—sometimes ignoring it altogether.

Her friends from the summer caution her to face her problems before catastrophe strikes. Is it too late to stop the destructive process Lacey has set in motion?

She went hot and cold all over. It was as if he'd shone a light into some secret part of her heart and something dark and ugly had crawled out. She had rejected Jeff because she didn't want a sick boyfriend. She'd said as much to Katie at Jenny House.

"It's any sickness, Jeff. It's mine too. I hate it all. I know it's not your fault, but it's not mine either."

"I'll bet no one at your school knows you're a diabetic."

She said nothing.

"I'm right, aren't I?"

"It's none of your business."

"You know, Lacey, you're the person who won't accept that you have a disease. Why is that?"

She whirled on him. "How can you ask me that when you've just admitted that girls drop you once they discover you're a bleeder? You of all people should understand why I keep my little secret."

Lacey is also featured in the novels *Please Don't Die* and *A Season for Goodbye*.

$\mathcal{I}$F YOU WANT TO KNOW MORE ABOUT KATIE,

CHELSEA, AND LACEY, BE SURE TO READ

ON SALE NOW FROM BANTAM BOOKS
0-553-56265-7

Excerpt from *A Season for Goodbye* by Lurlene McDaniel
Copyright © 1995 by Lurlene McDaniel

Published by Bantam Doubleday Dell Books for Young Readers
a division of Random House, Inc.
1540 Broadway, New York, New York 10036

*T*ogether again. It's been a year since Katie O'Roark, Chelsea James, and Lacey Duval shared a special summer at Jenny House. The girls have each spent the year struggling to fit into the world of the healthy. Now they're back, this time as "big sisters" to a new group of girls who also face life-threatening illnesses.

But even as the friends strive to help their "little sisters" face the future together, they must separately confront their own expectations. Katie must decide between an old flame and an exciting scholarship far from home. Chelsea must overcome her fear of romance. And Lacey must convince the boy she loves that her feelings for him can be trusted.

When tragedy strikes Jenny House, each of the girls knows that things can never be the same. Will Lacey, Chelsea, and Katie find a way to carry on the legacy of Jenny House? Can their special friendship endure?

"Over here!" Katie called. "I found it."

Chelsea and Lacey hurried to where Katie was crouched, digging through a pile of dead leaves. The tepee was partially buried, and Chelsea held her breath, hoping that the laminated photo and Jillian's diamond stud earring were still tied to it.

"It's come apart," Katie said, lifting up the twigs in three parts. But from the corner of one of the sticks, the laminated photo dangled, and from its center the diamond caught the afternoon sunlight.

The photo looked faded, but Amanda still smiled from the center of their group. Chelsea felt a lump form in her throat. These days, she and Katie and Lacey looked older, more mature, healthier too. But Amanda looked the same, her gamine smile frozen in time. And ageless.

Katie took the photo from Lacey's trembling fingers. "We were quite a bunch, weren't we?"

$\mathcal{Y}$OU CAN READ MORE ABOUT
MANY OF YOUR FAVORITE CHARACTERS FROM
THE ONE LAST WISH BOOKS IN

ON SALE NOW FROM BANTAM BOOKS
0-553-57109-5

Excerpt from *Reach for Tomorrow* by Lurlene McDaniel
Copyright © 1999 by Lurlene McDaniel

Published by Bantam Doubleday Dell Books for Young Readers
a division of Random House, Inc.
1540 Broadway, New York, New York 10036

$\mathcal{K}$atie O'Roark is thrilled to learn that Jenny House is being rebuilt. After the fire last year, Katie thought she could never return to the camp, where she spent the summers with young men and women like her who faced medical odds that were stacked against them. But thanks to Richard Holloway's efforts, Katie and her longtime friends Lacey and Chelsea will work as counselors once again. They'll be joined by Megan Charnell, Morgan Lancaster, and Eric Lawrence, who are newcomers to Jenny House but who have experienced the generosity of the One Last Wish Foundation.

It's not until Katie arrives at camp that she discovers that Josh Martel, her former boyfriend, is also a counselor. Katie and Josh broke up a year ago, when Katie decided to go away to college. Being near Josh again brings back a flood of old emotions for Katie. And when Josh confronts unexpected adversity, Katie knows she has to work out her feelings for him. Through the heart transplant she underwent years ago, Katie miraculously received a gift of new life. Now she must discover how to make the most of that precious gift and choose her future.

She stopped. By now tears had filled her eyes and her heart felt as if it might break. She truly believed that God had heard her prayer. What she did not know was whether or not he would grant her request. Against great odds, God had given her a new heart when she'd desperately needed one. And he had brought Josh into her life as well. She believed that with all her heart and soul. Now there was nothing more she could do except wait. And have faith.

Katie lifted her arms in the moonlight in supplication to the heavens.